Lame and Liminal

ruben encontrado

I'd like to dedicate this book to all the lost loved ones. I have been making phone calls to your current residence my entire life, but the line is always busy. I hope all is well.

To everyone who has supported me, thank you. To everyone who has strung me along, thank you. To everyone who has tried to bring me down, thank you.

We've all lost too much too quickly.

Preface: Somewhere Land

It is unclear if I have abandoned the world or if it has abandoned me.

I have a unique ability to build bridges for others and burn them for myself. My stories have the answers others need, as for me I am just spitting cherry seeds onto the highway. Coming up with another story as to why I should accept something superficial over what is genuine.

Who could I be if my stimulation wasn't always leading to a predictably surprising crash?

The only thing that is abundantly clear to me is that I wasn't built for this world. No, I was built to live under the stars as frequently as possible. To move in accordance with the movement of time. To wander from east to west to north to south. To listen to the bugs. Observe the birds. Feel the wind. Allow their great cosmic compass to guide me where it shall. If only it were different.

This is the type of freedom I long for. But how can one have freedom without any power? I don't know how long I have been asleep for, but it seems as though it has been long enough. I don't recognize this world or the people in it. The love I thought I had was an idea planted in my heart. It bloomed wonderful roses in my mind, but now that I know what I know I can't stop thinking of the thorns that have pricked my throat.

It is only when my message comes from a pure source that the wounds of my past indecisions are lathered with marmalade. Whatever the fuck that even means.

These stories are drawn off intricate emotional states, but are not based on any person or people in specificity. I give characters my worse attributes and the best attributes of others. Usually in some form of exaggeration to hopefully convey some larger meaning. Or no meaning at all. Because these are fiction. A.K.A made up. Extracted from weird space in my mind until I got this feeling that "Okay, I think I am done.". And that's the story. I just begin somewhere and end somewhere. I hope the ride is as cool for you as it is for me.

There was a man and a woman

There was a man and a woman. Like the countless that there are, but their connection to each other made them different then the rest. They were in love. Not shallow pond, but deep ocean. As if they were born for the sole purpose of being within one another's presence.

She was creative and outgoing with her passions but reserved with her opinions. Though she had many, she just figured her paintings spoke for themselves and didn't care to best someone in conversation. To prove she was right when she knew she was. It was a bother. She found people very infrequently wavered from their opinions. Especially when they were wrong.

He was analytical, knew what he liked and that was fine by him. He had been hurt too many times, so he shelved his heart. He had stories and jokes and opinions that were locked and loaded, to cover from getting into the meat of himself. This kept him socially ambiguous, but if the event were too large or the interaction too long, he became crippled by the anxiety of being exposed. Not that he would expose his true self to anyone other than himself. It was only when his finite social battery was exhausted was he forced to remember how much he was actually avoiding. Only willing to allow people in on a surface level because he was on the surface himself.

These two opposites seemed to be unlikely matches, but when they were apart, they were sick to their stomach. At some point they both had become more their love and less themselves. Love is the most vicious thing there was, is, and ever will be. When it all happened was unclear, but people wanted to be around them. Their love radiated and consumed a room. They would be with groups and only see each other. He would play with her hair, and she would tease him in a way that strangers couldn't help but blush.

But when they would get home, the walls were filled with her paintings. Her books. Her passion consumed a shared safe space. He felt smaller and smaller, but she could find no logical reason to restrict herself. She had few philosophies, but the few she adopted were seen as absolute. One of them was that her happiness could spread happiness. The apartment adored with her heart only made her passion grow. She thought her passion would reflect on him, but instead it buried him. She had forgotten that people rarely change their mind. An artist's philosophies are circumstantial and convenient. Love can be too invasive, it bypasses the philosophies we keep close to the chest because love occurs within the chest. He would see her paintings and her books, just to retreat into the mountain of questions that he thought he escaped when he found their love. The irony was her paintings and books that buried him, had the answers to his questions, but pride is a sorrowful thing.

Once they had a big blow-up argument. Well, more than once but this blow up had started at lunch and didn't end until months later. A celebrity had bought her painting, "Portrait of loneliness", and he drained her of her feelings. It was a painting of a hyper realistic old man she had seen in passing. She came home ecstatic, for it was a work that felt like a long awaited break from doing regular commission work. All she wanted to do was share the news with the only person she cared to share the news with, but he was at work. He was being passive aggressive again, not being able to leave the stresses of his high rise corporate career at work. He would come to his desk and tell her that he "wouldn't do it like that. Oh, not like that either. That's not it either. I'd show you how to do it, but I just have so much work to do today. Nope, that's not it either.". He hovered over his desk for an hour before his lunch break. Then when he mentioned that he was going to lunch, he would invite her. They had a lengthy conversation around the idea of him but did not include him in the details. He ate his chicken and rice somewhat pretending he wasn't there either. Getting lost in his chew. She was on the top floor of excitement and he was in the basement. Their conversation contained the distance. She waited for him to ask the source of her joy, but he never did. She went back to the apartment feeling guilty about her happiness. He took the elevator back fatigued and struggling to assign value.

So, after he returned to his desk from the long conversation and consumption, he felt unmotivated to work. Which only increased his depression on his commute back . He walked up the hill in a painful silence knowing he will repeat this walk tomorrow, but tomorrow will be filled with the dread that accompanied making up yesterday's work. Assuming he allowed himself to get to it.

He put his key in the door wanting nothing other than to sleep, but knowing they still needed groceries. But groceries weren't on her mind. She wanted him to be excited for her. She only wanted his excitement. She figured she'd cut right to it.

"Okay. I have good news. Do you want to sit down?"

"Hold on. Give me a minute to get settled."

"Okay. Sorry. How was your day?"

"Agh...I don't want to talk about it."

"Oh, no. Honey. What happened? Is everything okay?"

"Yah, it's fine. I just didn't get a lot of work done. Richard was doing that again."

"Why don't you just tell him to fuck off already?!"

"We have to work together."

"See that's why I could never do what you do. It's less the mundane of the office and more the type of people controlled by that mundane."

"Yah, I know. You have mentioned that before."

"Well, I am sorry you had a bad day. Would me having a good day make things better or worse?"

"I don't know. I am sure I am overthinking and tired. Tell me. How was your day?"

"Okay. SO. I had ThE MOST INCREDIBLE day ever. Literally the most incredible. Oh my god, I just don't even know where to begin."

"Probably, the beginning."

"Alright. Alright. Don't get an attitude with me just because I had a good day. You know not everyone works a job they hate."

"I don't hate my job."

"Then how would you describe your current state? And let me ask you, are you excited for work tomorrow?"

"We aren't talking about me. What happened today?"

She proceeded to tell him about how this well-known celebrity purchased her painting, "Portrait of loneliness.". She said it made him cry as soon as he laid eyes on it and he said that he "just needed to have it.". He was so generous that she had her rent money for this month, the next, and partially the one after. And it was only the sixth. This one purchase would open up so much time for her to explore her heart and soul. Expressing it all over the canvas with swift strokes of her brush. Maybe that she truly felt creative liberty not burdened by the social restraints that necessitated money she could finally create her masterpiece.

"That's really wonderful, baby."

"Seriously?"

"What did I say?"

"It's not what you said. It's how you said it. Don't think I don't know you. We have been living together for too long. I know when you aren't being genuine."

"I said that it was really wonderful."

"It's obviously wonderful! That's not the point. I would just wish that you could understand that. It's a wonderful experience for anyone but I am not anyone. I am yours. Why can't it be more than wonderful for you?!"

"Here we go."

"Oh, don't act like we have been here before. Like you know where it's going. It's pretentious and doesn't suit you."

"What is pretentious? Not being enough? Because that is the only thing that happens repeatedly. I am just never enough."

This was the normal course of their argument. They would usually find some solution. They would be so relieved that they had survived another successful argument. That they had each other once more, that they needed to have each other once more. Going into a frenzy of love making. They were compelled by the re-unification of their emotional selves to unify their physical selves. But the passion led them astray. Never allowing the dust to settle, clouding their emotions as they transitioned from two to one. They'd finish and just lay there.

On this day the part where sex gets stirred never arrived. Rather she said something that could never be taken back.

"I don't need you."

"What? What the fuck?"

"Oh, stop being dramatic. All I am saying is I don't need you. Not because I don't *need* you. I want you, there is a difference. I just don't need anyone."

What she wished she had said was, I don't need this version of you. Or, I'd rather not be with anyone then be with this version of you. But she didn't, she said, I don't need you. A subtle difference which means it's suffering will fall silently. That was when he started building his wall. Not a figurative wall, but a literal one. The following morning, he woke up next to her. Her delicate back turned to him. He dragged his palm across it like it would be the last time.

He then went to the local hardware store and purchased two pallets of bricks, six bags of ready-mix cement, a handful of wood studs, some three-sixty wheels, and a harness. He built an octagon base with the wood studs. At each of the connecting points attaching a three-sixty wheel. He then began to lay out the bricks. Building rows on each side. When the bricks of the octagon he was building were about waist high, she woke up with drool on her satin pillow. She heard the slap and slide of cement being applied with a steel spatula.

"The fuck are you doing??"

"Well, I just figured...you know so much more about life than I do. It was about time I did something creative."

"Okay,,, but what are you doing?", she rubbed her eyes. It was too much to witness before her morning coffee.

"It's an expression on the corruption of the world. We could look at this part as prep work. My muse will be time."

"Damn,,, that's deep.", she thoroughly understood that she was in love with a fucking moron.

"Yah, I called work."

"Okay. What did they say?"

"I told them I am going to take two weeks off for shoulder surgery and then for the next six months I am going to work from home."

"You are going to work from home!?", all she thought of was her masterpiece that needed her attention.

"Yah, it's not a big deal is it? I just feel passionate about this piece. Do you mind helping me for the next few months while I execute it?"

"What do you mean help you?"

His plan was to encapsulate himself in "the wall". Surround himself in red bricks for an undisclosed amount of time. It was a creative rebellion against the way our society over stimulates. All he needed her to do was to hand him food and talk to him every now and then. Of course, it would also imply taking the bucket filled with his waste and dumping it into the toilet. He had created a peephole for his cellphone and laptop chargers to be able to slip through. He was going to work and live stream the whole thing.

She was hesitant but ultimately agreed because she loved and trusted him. She also loved the idea of closing the gap that their recent arguments had created between them. Having the opportunity to support him at anything felt like an opportunity to make amends for what she had said. She had said "I don't need you.", but couldn't admit that it was a lie. What she wished she had said "I don't need who you currently are. I need the man that I know is somewhere in there.", but she didn't say that, so though his idea didn't make sense to her. She wanted to support it.

He spent three whole days building and preparing. It needed to be big enough to fit a small table for him to work and eat. Big enough to fit a chair for him to sit and work at. Big enough to fit a bed for him to sleep. He ended up finding that his one-bedroom apartment was limiting his creative endeavor. He decided that the desk and the chair were over kill and that he would just do this project laying down. The brick octagon ran from floor to ceiling and at it's widest allowed for a twin blow up mattress to fit snug.

When sealing the last brick, she watched him place it. But just before he did,

"Are you sure?"

"No, but this is what I am doing."

"Okay. What about food and water?"

"These bricks over here...", they were spray painted black. A 3x3 square of brick had a piece of thin wood beneath the final row. There was a 2x4 vertical to his left and her right on the inside. The piece below was on hinges and the cement was left unsealed. He unhitched a dead bolt and the bricks swung inward giving a window at about waist height. "...it should be enough room for me to pass you my bucket and for you to pass me whatever I need.". She let out a deep breath, something about the practicality of this window made the reality of his big red well as immense as it was.

"How long are you going to do this for?"

"For as long as I can. I'll do pushups and run-in place to stay fit. I'll still have my half of rent."

"Okay. I support you. I just...Do you think you have a time frame? I just this project isn't just affecting you ya'know. I just could really use an end date. Something to look forward to.". It was mid-July, and they had their lease until November.

"I'll come out in time to help pack."

"Okay. I'll miss you."

"I am not going anywhere."

"I know but still. It feels like you are."

He smiled and sealed the last brick. He then shut the window. Clicked open his phone and went live. He had made a burner account. @the_man_trapped_in_america. He didn't say a word, just propped his phone in a corner, opened his laptop and began working. The wire ran through, and his live stream was never not running. People became infatuated. The first few hours there were only a few viewers but by the end of the week thousands were tuning in to watch him do nothing. About a few months in, packages began to arrive at the door. Sponsors were sending him clothes to wear. Protein bars, bed comforters, pajamas. One tech start up even sent him a laptop.

Fan accounts started to pop up. Not for the mystery man immersed in the red bricks, but of the occasional feminine hands that would deliver food. Occasionally delivering books that he would begin and get bored of. @mrs.mystery_manos. @the_nutritionist. One person asked on the stream, "if the hands were only for providing delivery services?". He was insulted and finally spoke which had not happened since he had told her that he wasn't going anywhere. At first, she thought he was taking a spiritual vow of silence, but as he began to pass her notes with his filled buckets or empty plates or both, she began to feel something about the bricks had given him the inability to speak. Something about that truth would slowly remove her tongue as well. Maybe it was the fact that he never looked out the window, only handed things to her. She hadn't seen his face and refused to join the stream. On the day that this one follower made a facetious comment he spoke up, and things changed. He said her name and that her hands helped him but they were mainly for creating great paintings.

The household had never seen such success. He was making his regular income and had basically an additional salary coming in from social media and sponsors while her paintings were constantly being shipped out. The hundreds that had occupied closet space were suddenly gone and she was in demand. There was a problem. All she wanted to do was complete the piece of her dreams. Her magnum opus. She bought a large 48x48 canvas and countless tubes of paint. In the swiftness of her brushstrokes, she would finally understand all that was once misunderstood. She not only wanted to do this piece before all the commission requests she was receiving, but she also felt a compulsion to do it. Compulsion combined with inability always equates to repulsion. She began to feel an extreme nausea at the forefront of her destiny. Every time she opened her sketchbook or began to paint or would brainstorm, all she could produce were wells and red brick. Her ability to create had been stripped from her. She had hundreds of requests waiting for her with outlandish price tags attached to them. She felt maybe she could ignore the requests. Maybe art is so subjective that she can produce what she produced and claimed to have their request in mind. If they didn't get it, then they didn't get it. It's not the responsibility of the agent to control the emotions produced by the object, rather the only responsibility was to the creation itself. She began shipping out canvas's of varied sizes, going through countless red tubes of paint. She'd paint wells. A single brick. A series of bricks. Sometimes the canvas was just red. Despite what you may think, people received it well. She had immeasurable amounts of success. So much so, that Mister Mystery Mustache head of the Museum of Modern Art called her off his personal phone.

"Listen lady, I have been in this industry aloooooong time.", he said with a nasely throat. A specific characteristic of those who have been in the industry along time. "I know when someone has got it and you've got it. It would be a disservice to see your talent go to waste. Let's put on a show. Let's put together an exhibit. Can you have twenty pieces done by the twenty fifth?"

It was the first of September when he had called. She agreed without thinking twice. As soon as she got off the phone, she went into the other room to tell the only person she cared to tell. She was banging on the 3x3 square of black painted brick. It sounded like dough being prepared for bread, just less shaking. If she was watching the stream, she would have known he was taking a nap. She would have also seen how skinny he had gotten. How long his beard and hair were getting. But there was one thing that she was certain of was that he was in desperate need of a shower.

After waiting for a while, she began to yell the news. Suddenly this event that was intended to have a soft launch, had all the publicity it would ever need. The stream began to explode as she imploded on the adjacent side of the coarse wall. It's stubbles dragging against her back as she slid down in her collapse.

"I never imagined how this project of yours would change us. I don't know if you can hear me, but I have been working at this for a long time. I am grateful for all the ways you have helped me. I just need you differently. It would mean a lot if you came. You still have twenty-five days, until the event, but yah. I miss you. It's funny, kinda, but if you saw the paintings I am selling. I can only paint wells, and bricks, and red. Anyways, I need you. I don't know what you set out to accomplish, but I think you did it."

He didn't hear a word of it, but his viewers did. They pitied her and judged him.

The next twenty-five days were spent as the previous months were. Her cooking for two, dumping his waste, and then going into the bedroom to paint. The 48x48 canvas resting on the easel almost taunting her. The edges with insecure strokes of red. Strong at their origin and fading out well before they can get to the center. Creating a teardrop of white in a sea of red canvases.

She painted three paintings a day. Each looking like the other but on day twenty she had plenty of paintings to be shipped out and displayed. Then as she was cleaning her supplies she found an old water color he once did for her. She looked at it. It wasn't even on a canvas just a thick piece of paper. A sky blue lightly placed by the brush, with two tiny birds flying. One chasing the other. "Two birds in a pale blue sky", was it's inscription on the back.

After loading her paintings, she found a glimpse of herself again. The day for the gallery was here and he still made no attempts to come outside, and that was it. The gallery made her feel like she was alone at sea. It went well, but that wasn't the point. The next day she packed some clothes, brushes, and other tools, and she left. She was refusing to watch the live.

The art gallery went well and some of her pieces sold for more than anticipated, but he wasn't there. She found herself scanning the room, half participating in conversations, and staying close to the entrance. Him not showing up felt like betrayal, but she couldn't help but feel pity.

She spent a week away when she finally decided to look at the stream. It was then she saw the number of viewers had dropped from the thousands to a few hundred. That wasn't the concerning part, that was almost expected, what was concerning was that he had turned the knife on himself. He was peeling layers off his thigh and consuming himself. Sustenance was more important than well being.

He was about to cut off another pieces of his thigh when he heard the jingling of keys and then the creak of a door. There was a thump and then a pause. She had returned with a sledgehammer.

You Go To The Dentist Often

Everytime I go to the dentist, the same exact guy is sitting in the lobby. We always sit across from each other. I am not sure if I wear the same thing each time, but he definitely does.

He is always wearing a teenage mutant ninja turtle shirt, a light vest, and has his laptop. Always working on some kind of script.

Three thoughts always come to mind. The first, I used to love teenage mutant ninja turtles. The second, I should tell him I am a writer too. The third, when people pull off vests, they really pull them off. I am unfortunately not someone who can.

Ah, the fourth, I fucking hate the dentist. It's an important staple to the hygiene and the well being of our community. I just rather not if I didn't have to. My friend says it's a pride thing.

He always looks at me. Then writes something down. I always wonder if I am inspiring a character. This time I went somewhere weird.

As I sat across from this man, I wondered if he was me. Or I was him. Maybe he was writing his story and I am just a narrative brought to life by the images in his head. Like I was a figment in his imagination. So vivid and tragic, that it felt real. But it only felt real. It was something different. I had this eerie feeling of not caring. Like it wasn't important though a part of me felt like it was really important. It's real enough.

If I am just one of his character, then what are my rules. What can you do when you are just a character in someone else's story? Damn it! I am thinking about her, again–

"Sebastian, they are ready for you."
Root canal or routine check-up, they will tell me in a minute.

Life Can Be a Comedy

The line at the pharmacy is so long today. I have plenty of meds, but I like picking mine up a half hour after they've been refilled. Less possibility of the pills being tampered with.

Good only one more person now.

I am next up.

Blue chocolate bars. Walls are filled with shelves of brown color. They are metallic and have dull corners. The walls are light blue. Like the sky at four o'clock in the spring.

Some of the people have white coats, others are wearing a navy button down, and the rest seem to not care. Or they care but in a different way.

The counter is plastic or some strange material but definitely not the granite it's been painted to look like. The person behind me is chewing on his gum very loudly. The only thing louder is the music in his headphone. I hear that. The shifting and sliding of pills being put into bottles and bottles being put into bags. Printers printing prescriptions. Phone calls being made in the back. The counter is shouting for a price check. The old woman before me is breathing heavy. The girl behind the counter is checking me out. No. She is checking out the gum guy behind me. Better that way.

I am up. I provide the necessary information. They tell me they will get it. They don't get it. It will be ready soon. I refuse to move. I threaten to make a scene. In a few moments my pills are available.

I am walking out declartively. There are cars whizzing by on the street. People talking outside of storefronts. There is a general rumble that is pleasant to take apart. Am I a Karen?

No, I just needed my pills. Oh my god, I'm a Karen. Should I go back and apologize? No way. That's just gonna piss them off more. I'll just change my pharmacy.

I am parked four blocks ahead. I thought the pharmacy was going to take longer so I paid for four hours of parking.

I have always wanted to try this pizzeria. Normally eating out isn't for me. You never know what's in the ingredients. But I have confidence on my side. I was an ass hole. I am remorseful. But for a brief instance it felt good. That's gotta be why people are ass holes. When you don't think about the effect on others putting someone down feels good? Sometimes we are starving for some good. It's still better not to be an ass hole, but we have moments of weakness. It's a difficult world. I should just still be kind.

Everytime I go down into the dungeon to think, no matter what path I follow it's either empathy, love, or compassion. It's just so hard to embody all of that, when your kindness is always doubted. We live in a difficult time. Hurt is going around and the only thing spreading faster are instructions on how not to hurt.

When I open the door, the warm waft of the pizza hits me in the face. I'm thinking buffalo chicken. Oh fuck that, a chicken roll. Shake my head of the idea. You came here for pizza. The woman behind the counter seems entertained by your distress.

"Buffalo chicken slice and a margarita, please. And thank you."

She slides them into the oven. Resting her palm on the counter and pulling her phone to her face. What if I wanted to have a conversation with you? You just missed out on human connection for a dopamine rush. Her loss. I know how cool I am. So cool. Damn—

I knocked over the tip jar. I helped her clean up the coins then slipped two bucks into it. After repeating sorry, many times. She offered to bring me the slice. "Just have a seat, sweetie.".

Why'd she call me sweetie? She doesn't know me. Is the assumption that I am bitter and in need of some sugar? Or that I am in fact sweet and in need of some diluting? Both of these questions feel nonsensical and irrelevant. And oddly inappropriate. She is cute, but I could never.

She brings the two slices over to me. Places them down with a cup of water. And I am salivating.

"You from around here?"

"Ten minutes away. I just don't get out much."

"Well, get out more. You have a cute face, I'd remember you."

I didn't say anything as she walked behind the counter. The last words she uttered were, "Enjoy.".

I hope our children have her hair. The pizza was delicious. I thought that the spice from the chicken might make the flavor of the margarita dull. But I also didn't want to risk eating cold chicken. I started with the buffalo.

As I was swallowing my final bite, a man walks into the pizzeria. I must emphasize that the entire pizzeria was empty. I was certain because I stood up to confirm my suspicion. Suspicious because out of all the available seats this dirty man chose to sit across from me. I took the first bite of the margarita without taking my eyes off of him.

Finally, I said something.

"Hello."

"Shut The Fuck Up.". Of course. Precisely. Why didn't I think of that?

Then I remember something from a really long time ago. A memory I haven't seen in a while. One that I haven't even thought of. I wonder how they are doing?

"I am not gonna sit with a stranger. Introduce yourself or find somewhere else to sit."

"Ralph."

"Ralph what?"

"Ralph Shut The Fuck Up"

"Well, Ralph Shut The Fuck UP what do you do for a living?"

"Minding my business."

"They hiring? Right—sorry. Bad joke."

"You gonna finish your pizza?"

"You want my pizza?", I was about half way done with the margarita. It was still in my hand.

"Can I have it? Yes or no?"

"Dude, I would have bought you a fresh slice."

"Really?"

"No, fuck you, eat my scraps, bitch."

I quickly made my way out of the pizzeria. As I looked in through the window, I had this feeling Mr.Ralph Shut The Fuck Up kinda liked me. Or he was going to kill me the next time he saw me. Either way I admired such incredible passion.

I am walking slowly down the sidewalk towards my car. This guy is fixing the chain on his son's bike. Three people are having a smoke on the corner. A car speaker is playing reggaton. Maybe a block away from the car, there is a round table with an old woman hovering over it.

She smiles at me as I get closer. Then right before I get to the table she turns her back. The table is lined evenly with dead mice. I hold the image of it for a second and there is no good angle to process it.

I am lost until I get to my car. I sit on the driver seat. Look at myself in the mirror and think, *I am never going outside again.*

But then I am overcome with laughter. What a spectacular world.

A Lighthouse in The Sky

When the old man in the sky was a young man on the ground, he prayed to God every morning, evening, and night. The way his father did. The way his grandfather did. The words his grandmother showed him. The posture his mother displayed.

One day before they worked on the grape farm–the grapefarm his grandfather had inherited from his grandfather–he prayed to God by the river. The long and winding river that lead to the ocean.

On his knees and eyes to the sky, "My lord, I know I am young, but my faith is strong. My lord, I know I haven't prayed enough, but I believe. Please, show me a sign. I don't doubt you, but I need to see. My faith has been tested and I am in need of resolve."

At that moment a fish leaped from the river. A finch in the tree sang an incomplete song. A fisherman with his rod on his shoulder came walking down the path. He was barefoot in overalls. His straw hat was just as tired as his skin. He was young, but his skin and eyes showed he had lived a hundred lives. He was whistling an incomplete tune.

"You won't find what you're looking for on your knees. Swimming is fun, but a boat is better.", he said as he walked by the devout boy. He continued walking on. In the silence of an incomplete music the boy on the ground began to contemplate.

He heard his duty call him using his grandfather's voice. The grapes wouldn't pick themselves. The rows were in need of watering.

The boy on the ground worked on autopilot. His body going through the motions that it had gone through since he began to remember. But his ghost was elsewhere. It was trapped by the sight of the leaping fish. It was trapped in the incompleteness of the music. Lost in the words of a stranger. The boy on the ground asked for a sign and things had changed. He couldn't deny it. The question was, is this God's doing or mere coincidence? Is there a difference?

That night at dinner the boy on the ground's mother said grace. The portions were served and each person said what they were grateful for in the order of seniority. When it was the boy on the ground's turn he froze like ice that he had never seen.

"Find it, my boy.", the grandfather said.

"I'd like to build a boat.". Everyone was taken back. The grandma was the first to speak up.

"My sweet champagne, we are telling the lord what we are grateful for."

"I am saying what I am grateful for. I'd like to explore God's river and ocean."

There was a silence. The mother picked up her food to move her food around on her plate. The grandfather was the next to speak. Everyone listened because everyone outwardly knew all the decisions needed to be approved by the oldest man. Everyone inwardly knew the oldest man needed the approval of his wife.

"I'll give you supplies and a half a year. If you're serious get to work tomorrow. If after six months that boat sinks, then it's back to the vineyard. You'll need to work double time, my boy. To make up for lost time of course. If after six months that boat floats, then we will give you food and push you from our shores with prayers in our heart."

The grandmother smiled. She approved of the proposition. The grandfather knew she would they had been married so many decades. They no longer required words to communicate.

The father was somewhat in disbelief at his own father's attitude. The mother couldn't contain the excitement in her eyes.

In less than a week the boy had a design for the boat finished. He called for his family to watch the launch. He paddled out in the small boat. The family clapped for him at the shore as he made it out past the reeds.

The boat took on water. Panic insued. Before the boy on the water could resolve the problem the boat sunk. He was soaked. The family laughed deeply. When the boy swam to shore the only thing he said to his mother was, "I'll start building a better boat tomorrow.".

The next boat took two weeks to build. Made it a little further off the banks of the river, but like the first sunk like a stone.

The boat that followed took three weeks to construct. This one didn't even make it as far as the first. The family's laughter began to fade out as the soaked boy on the ground began to lay his fists to the trunk of a tree. The grandmother seeing his frustration remembered how good she was at drawing before she was a mother.

Prayer had taught the boy on the ground less about the words he recited and more about the nature of devotion. The importance of consistency. The depths of dedication.

Actually, what led him to doubt and the desire for resolve were the words. They gave him very little peace and often left him mystified.

After five weeks the boy was ready to test his newest construction. It was his proudest work. He was learning with each design. His father was excited for him. His mother was nervous it would sink. His grandmother was hopeful. His grandfather was growing tired.

The boat launched. "Lord be my light.", the boy on the water said to himself. He paddled slowly. Past the reeds. Further than he has ever been. He is catching the current! The boy on the water felt like his heart had been hooked. His body was being pulled in the direction of adventure. He never felt so alive.

He dropped his paddle and stood on his feet. He shouted as loud as he could. Raised his paddle toward victory. The adventure he felt spread to his family watching from the banks. He is going to do it!

When the boy on the water began to trust his excitement, the current began to ebb him left. He noticed too late. He shoved the paddle into the water but his fate was sealed there was no redirecting. He crashed into a large stone, took on water, and in an instant was submerged.

He swam back over to his family. They all looked at him not knowing what to say. He brought his knees to his chest and gave them his back. His eyes became fixed on a location. The water just passed through the field of his vision.

"Dinner will be ready soon, my little champagne.", she kissed his cheeks.

"We are very proud of you.", his father said with his arm wrapped around his wife.

Everyone left besides the grandfather. He sat next to his grandson on the wet dirt to his right. There was a finch singing an incomplete song.

"When I was a boy, I wanted to grow the world's largest grape. I even believed God wanted me to do this. I told my family and they gave me time to chase my dream. It's important to try. If you try and fail, well then you know, my boy. If you try and succeed, then you have succeeded. The point is I see my dedication in you. I tried constantly watering the grapes. I tried depriving the grapes. I tried adding sugar to the water. I slept outside so the grapes could eat my dreams. But after months of the grapes being the same size I had to accept that grapes are grapes. That grape farmers are grape farmers. They are meant for vineyards not the ocean. Accept your failures as a sign from God, my boy.". He placed a comforting hand around his shoulder.

The Grandfather got up leaving the boy on the ground with the river, the incomplete song of the finch, and his failures. The boy thought that in his pursuit of God's message to him he experienced more doubt than what made him seek in the first place.

He wanted to cry, but no tears ever came. The boy looked to the sky once more preparing himself to let go, he heard another song coming from across the river. A fisherman in a straw hat with bare feet. He stopped singing, looked at the boy, and waved. Then disappeared into the bush. One more boat, the boy on the ground thought.

After he cleaned up, dinner was waiting. When it became his turn to declare what he was grateful for he said, "The river.". His father asked him why.

"I work by it everyday and it's quiet, but it's not. The finches in the trees sing incomplete songs. I can't tell if the river is singing, but if it is the song is complete."

The grandfather was shocked by the boy on the ground's wisdom. The mother moved her food around on the plate. The grandmother had a glow in her eyes. She was a mischievous old woman and was up to something. The grandfather could tell she was plotting, but what she was plotting eluded him.

"Meet me by the river after dinner.", the grandmother said to the boy on the ground. They ate in silence.

After dinner the grandmother and the boy on the ground walked out to the river. The moon was very bright this night, so they didn't need a lantern.

"There is something I'd like to show you.", the grandmother said as she reached into her shawl. She handed the boy a handful of papers.

"My family didn't inherit the vineyard. I chose it when I chose your grandfather. My family didn't believe in God. I chose it when I chose your grandfather. My family believed in something called mathematics. Understanding the world through what can be measured instead of what cannot be measured. I have accepted both in my life and if your boat doesn't work with these designs. I'd love to show you the way. What can be measured and what cannot aren't that different."

The boy gazed deeply at the lines on the page. It was becoming clearer by the moment. The grandmother spoke again as she saw the curiosity growing within the boy on the ground.

"The same way I instructed you in prayer; I will instruct you on how to build a boat. I have put it in terms you will understand." Each line was explained in the length of reeds.

"Tomorrow I will help you find the perfect reed to use for this design. We will need to begin before I have to work the vineyard."

The boy on the ground didn't know what to say. He hugged his grandmother beneath the moonlight. As he felt her warmth he listened to the river at night. It somehow sounded clearer in the dark. He was now certain the river had a song.

After morning prayers, they were patient, but eventually found the perfect reed. The grandmother gave him a blessing. He began to cut wood.

He worked with precision for weeks. The father frequently visited him after his day on the vineyard. One of these days a cool breeze passed for the entirety of his work. The father's brisk hair would slap on to his forehead, keeping him chilled all day. He went to visit his son, the boy on the ground, when he saw the designs on the floor. He picked them up to analyze them closer. He knew it was the work of his mother.

He also knew that though his son, the boy on the ground, had the ambition and the will, he could never achieve what he wanted to do next. Not alone.

With his hairs still standing from the chilled breath of the sky, he picked up a piece of wood and held it steady. He said to his son, the boy on the ground, to, "Nail it here.".

The father and son would work on the boat everyday. He would arrive, exhausted, seeing his son, exhausted, but not giving up. They didn't speak much. It was understood that this type of work required the prayer of quiet.

Eventually the grandmother would bring out their dinner and extra lanterns. She would sit on the floor as they worked, and eat. Then when they would stop to eat, she would get to work. When everyone was done eating, all hands were working. Until they had no choice but to sleep. The mother always drinking her tea in the doorway, making sure grandpa was okay, while supporting them from afar.

Many nights, especially in the end, the three of them would lay upon the wet banks and sleep beneath the stars. The only thing to be heard is the complete song of the river and the incompete music of silence.

No words were ever spoken but each silently considered one another to be the many faces of God's love.

Eventually, when the mother knew that the grandfather was sleeping, she would run over to them. She was a natural seamstress and began diligently working on the sail.

In no time the boat was ready to disembark, and the now grumpy grandfather never even witnessed a moment of it's construction.

Everyone filled the ship with supplies. It was clear that this time would be a success and the boy will be able to set sail.

He climbed upon the ship and they pushed him out. He guided it into the current. Locked it in the direction. As he turned to look back, his grandfather was waving from a top the bank. His dad jumped for joy, his mother cried as she clenched her chest, and the grandmother sat on the ground. She looked at her reflection in the water.

The boy on the ground became the boy upon the river.

A gust of wind came in and he was speeding towards the bay. The embankment to the right and the left became obtuse. The great ocean was opening up before him. He saw where the sky and the ocean met. The same sun he had seen his entire life was now an immaculate embodiment of something more. Suspended in all of it's grandiose.

He sailed towards it. Now that the decision is past him, he is realizing he knows nothing about anything. The only thing he knows is how to harvest grapes, how to be grateful, and how to build a boat. He will be at the mercy of his own inuition. An excellent guide that can only be refined through mistakes.

He made it past the bay. Before he knew it the land that he always had known dwindled behind him.

The days passed. He ate through his supplies quite quickly. His belly had demands, but so did his boredom. The boy on the ground, who became the boy on the river, who became the boy at bay, and is now the boy at sea. The excitment of that carried him at first.

But even the rich gloss of light that glides above the surface of the ocean becomes dull to a silent mind. Dull is the wrong word. It's a leap of acknowledgement. An internal recognition that if it glimmers there it glimmers in here. Beauty can only exist if you are brave enough to become it.

Another week went by. The boy didn't have enough food. His belly ached and he fed it with prayers. There was this spot at the head of the boat. He would sit there while resting his back on the wall. In deep states of frozen silence. Contemplating the song of the ocean. Trying to follow it's music inward to discover if it is complete or not.

Eventually too many days had passed. His young body began to decay. How vividly he could imagine his grandmother's meals.

He went inside to die on his cot. When he laid down in the bed, he heard a strange crunch. He raised the bed of feathers and beneath it were a bundle of reeds. Some string and a hook. The grip is the interweaving of vines from the vineyard.

A small letter from his grandfather:

"The vines are not going anywhere."

The boy in the setting sun dropped his line into the water. There was a bite. It put up a valiant fight, but in the end the boy at sea over took the large tuna. This large blue fish lay in his lap. Many thoughts ran through his head until he just behaved. Digging his teeth into the tuna. Bite after bite. Consuming it raw.

He slept well but woke up early. Throwing up uncontrollibally. When the vomiting ceased, his belly ached in soreness.

He began to eat the raw tuna, again. For some time he was alright as he slept the meal away, but when he woke the vomiting returned.

There was no more tuna to fill his belly. The day began to quake with imminent darkness. The boy decided to lay flat on his back. He watched as the stars slowly broke through the darkening sky. Were his family on that cool bank by the vineyard? Looking at the same set of stars? Before he knew it he was submerged into a weak sleep.

He awoke when water splashed on board. His ship was pointing toward light, but it was slamming into waves. Teetering upon chaos, as the ocean lifted him to the heavens, and slammed him down toward the unknown.

He grabbed on to what he could, but all efforts felt senseless against the wrath of a storm at sea. He stood wide enough to position of his footing. He placed his hand on his forehead and on his chest. He began to shout the prayer his grandmother had taught him.

"MERCY BE UPON ME.
MERCY BE UPON THE SOULS OF OTHERS
THAT WEAR MY FACE WHEN THEY WEAR SORROW.
I WILL HOLD YOU IN MY PRACTICE.
TO KNOW YOU IS TO KNOW ONESELF.
MERCY BE UPON ME.
I HAVE FOUGHT IN THE SPIRIT OF YOU
BUT YOUR COMPASS GUIDES ME TO TRECHEROY.
WHEN I ASK TO SHOW ME THE WAY.
YOU MAKE MY WAY MORE DIFFICULT.
IT IS ONLY AFTER TIME
THAT I SEE YOU IN LAUGHTER.
MERCY BE UPON ME.
I HAVE ASKED FOR STRENGTH
AND YOU HAVE GIVEN ME TRIALS.
HERE I STAND.
HERE I STAND.
HERE I STAND.
I WILL BE NOTHING, AT THE MERCY OF YOUR
COMMAND."

As the song of the ocean reached it's highest octave. He broke through the storm. Now in a pocket of light he stands alone and soaking wet. In the eye of the storm.

A golden voice runs up his spine and gives him an ultimatum.

"Die or be my slave?"

Without a single thought the boy began to steer his boat in the direction of the storm. As he did the eye became smaller and began to cyclone. The remaining light from the sun collapsed into a beam and then into nothing.

The front of the boat began to lift, again. Rising each time. Like a wild stallion raising it's hooves higher each time. Until finally…

The boat lifted up from the sea. He began to ride the wind. Being hurled closer and closer to the clouds. As he approached, the stom became more violent. Just when he thought he couldn't handle the storm any longer–he broke through the clouds.

He rose above. His boat gliding on top of the soft clouds. Even the aroma felt weightless.

His boat slowly moved along. The rain droplets quickly drying against the rays of sun now beaming down on the boy in the sky.

He looked out on the weightlessnes of it all. The boy understood as he looked out on the horizon, where the cloud of beds met the sun, that he had surrendered. He hoped it was God, but whoever was here–he was now at their mercy.

The silence felt different. It was like it made it's way through the floor boards. The boy in the sky heard his own pulse.

A body was in the nude. The boy in the sky had never seen a naked woman before, but he knew the body before him had more than just a man's parts.

She wore a crown of thorns around her waist. Upon her head was a mirrored halo. She sat on top of an orange squid. The tentacles coming together in a fist then pushing gravity back into the clouds. She just looked at the boy. Without moving his mouth the boy in the sky had understood what had been said.

Leave your name in the sea and come with me.

The boat seemed to be tethered to her squid. It traveled away from the horizon. At least, the one with the descending sun.

They traveled in this direction for three days and three nights. Then suddenly they came to the shore of a small island. It had a small house with many books. A cluster of reeds. A well. A row of grapes. A row of olives. There was a tight knit archipelago of stones leading toward a tall light house.

The being of sensuality, anointed the boy in the sky into a knight of the infinite resignation. The boy in the sky humbly accepted all that he did not understand.

The lighthouse is a guide back to here. As I continue to traverse the infinite, it's my duty as humble observant to select a lighthouse worker, when the other dies and returns.

You are the new lighthouse observer. It will require your prayers every morning and every night. Do not forget the prayer of quiet. This will keep the flames on. To guide me back here as a I traverse and observe.

The next time you will see me, in this form, you will be dying. You may ask me one question?

"What do you mean, return?", the knight of the infinite resignation said as he got off his boat. Dropping down on to the island that would be his home for some time.

When you die up here, you will return to your family on the vineyard. In the exact moment you heard the call. And you can choose then to answer the call like you did, or deny it. You will make the decision after a lifetime of solitude.

This being than looked at the knight of the infinite resignation directly. The weighlessness of his surroundings had become one with his breath. She kissed the knight of the resignation on the forehead. Forever gracing him with their eyes and ears.

Then they no longer were. And the knight was alone. Sorrowful even. But he feared what would happen if the lantern went out. So he would pray routinely. His diet consisted of the olives and grapes that never ran out.

He'd sit for hours on the island witnessing the prayers of his grandmother dissipate with his memories. He became so entranced in prayer and such a light diet that his prayer of quiet–the one he had forgotten he had learned with his father–became his continuous state of being.

The knight of the infinite resignation was uncertain of all things, but felt that the lighthouse had never shined brighter. That his connection with the lighthouse has deepened beyond compare.

Oddly enough, there is no wind here. The chimes are still, except for the moments he smacks them.

He decides to climb the stairs of the lighthouse for the first time. He ascends. Seeing an immense flame but it is deadly quiet. Not a single crackle or flap.

Out on the balcony all you saw was clouds in every direction. Then a finch came and landed on the black gothic railing. It sung an incomplete song. It was the first thing the knight of the infinite resignation had heard in years. Besides the occasional storm in the distance, or smack of the chime.

One of the prayer's from his forgotten childhood slipped out.
"The love of longing–
You slip through my fingers
While I feel your touch in my throat
Take me–for without you I am imperfect.
But with you I am accepted.
Grace me from above
And I will climb whatever ladder you offer."

The bird twisted it's head to the side as it looked at the adult man. Then it sung a complete song. It's strange the way an epiphany is nothing and also the most important moment.

The Knight of the infinite resignation, sprinted down the stairs and to his boat. His meditations had become so refined that he was able to guide it with his ghost.

It went out on to the bed of clouds. He looked inside the cabin and found the fishing pole made of reeds. At it's touch he heard the words, "consider your failures to be a sign from, God."

These were the only words the knight of the infinite resignation could remember from his past. The prayers just flowed out of him thoughtlessly. The words were nothing to him but a stone skipping upon the surface of water.

He sent his line into the clouds and with some time he would hook a finch by the heart. Then they were tethered and he would draw them in through the prayer of quiet. They would rise with the hook in their claw.

He would then recite a prayer to the little finch. The finch would sing a song in it's completion back.

This became the routine of the man who was aging. He'd engage with prayer in the morning. Make a sack of olives and grapes. Guide his boat out to the vast brushstrokes of creation. Hooking as many finches as he could. Reciting a prayer for them. Listening to them sing.

Then he would return to his island. And contemplate over the lighthouse.

This is how The Knight of the infinite resignation chose to spend his life. He lived to be surprisingly old.

On one warm evening, he decided to lay on the dirt of the island and engage in a different kind of prayer. To be nostalgic. The Knight of the infinite resignation didn't know if he accomplished anything with his life. The only thing he was certain of is that he was from somewhere that was further from the stars and closer to the ground.

The word ocean would occasionally come to mind, but the only imagine that could be conjured was a sea of white. The flame of the lighthouse went out as a gust came over the island.

The next thing he knew the knight of the infinite resignation was anointed. The woman carried a holy air. It was the last thing he would see. It had been so long that he had seen something new that he believed she was himself.

He became a knight of faith. He was walking down a dirt path by a river bank. Their is a boy coming up on your right. He is young and looks familiar but you don't know how. You are both listening to the incomplete song of the finch. In this passing moment, they both hear the remainder of the song in the wind. The boy by the river forgets it, but your under the shade of a straw hat; you remember. Now your surroundings are a symphony.

There is a woman in a doorway to your left. Some distance away. A man is walking towards her. An old man and woman are discussing something very intimately by the vines. You follow the song down the dirt path, never to see them again.

This is your call. You are wondering how you should answer. So instead you choose not to. You just begin to walk in whatever direction feels natural. Without warning you have become the boy on the ground again. You remember everything, but you don't recognize yourself. This supreme being embeds one ideal into your heart that will serve as the guide of your curiosity. *Could you be loved?*

What if Liberation Smacked You in the Face?

My dad rested his paw on my shoulder. My head was the same head it had always been, but in this instant an immeasurable weight had it fixed in a downward position. The ebb and flow of black waves etched into the wood table absorbed me.

"You don't understand, honey, this job was gonna get him out of this town. Now he is stuck with us.", my dad said while hovering above. Staring at my mother who is trying so hard to understand my disappointment. She leaning on the counter; waiting for the water to boil.

"Beeing *stuck* is not something I was considering. I just really liked this job. We did a lot of good for the world, but of course–"

"Of course, what?!", my father asks accusationally.

"This doesn't feel like the time for it."

"Speak your truth, son.", my mother touched her lips without taking her eyes off of my father. He now got eye level as he sat in the chair to my right. Resting his elbow on the table. His eyebrow scrunched; hoping I'd say what he thinks I am going to say.

"I am just gonna walk the dog."

"Oh, sweetie! The tea is almost ready. Let's work it out together."

"Let him go, honey. The kid is in the mood to run away from his problems. We know what happens when we get in the way of that."

Just let it roll off of you. Just let it roll off of you. You are bigger than your anger. You are bigger than your anger. You are deserving of peace.

"Let's go, Icarus.", the old boxer hoped off the couch. Met me by the door with a wagging tail. My smile hurt. As we left I heard my mother whisper with poison.

"Joaquin, you know he is sensitive, why do you do these things!?"

I shut the door and the old dog yanked at my shoulder. Icarus is still strong despite being nine years ago. They got him for me when we moved into this house.

The land is flat but it's surrounded by mountains of clary grey. When we moved in the foundation for a house to the left of us was built. This empty square whole still sits there. The intention was clearly there, but it doesn't look like they will ever build a home.

Before we break out of the cul de sac, he pees on the neighbors mailbox. The mailbox is black, the house is navy blue, and the porch is white. The old man stares at me from his bench, like I am the one pissing on his lawn.

Maybe, I should just quit. I mean, can I really say it's been worth it. No matter what I do, I end up being consoled (poorly) by my parents. No matter what I do, I can't stop staring at the highway beyond the trees.

I make a right at the corner. I usually have a route in mind, but it's a nice enough afternoon.

"Icarus, you're in charge. I'm following your lead. Show me your world, old fella."

At the corner he started sniffing toward the right. Then suddenly we are going left. There was a speech in Mexico City next week. New York in a month and Nepal the week after, for conferences. To elevate human consciousness through developments in Artificial Intelligence! I mean I was on the precipice of the new world! And all my parents see is me not wanting to spend time with them...

My neighbor has a MAGA flag on his front lawn. He is working on his truck with his son. They both wave at me. I wave back. Would they wave if they knew I was listening to Bad Bunny?

I've just always idolized revolutionary figures. Not because they were violent or cool or whatever. That didn't hurt, but I loved the idea of being an embodiment of change. So, no I don't want to be stuck. Not stuck with them, but in consistency. Waking up at the same time everyday. Having breakfast, going down to work with my dad, repeating the same variation of activities in the same variation of places, coming home to the same spot I have been for my whole life.

There is so much I want to see! So much I want to feel! So much I want to do for others! But when I tell my father this, he always gives me the same line about Kant never leaving his hometown. The predictability had made me quiet…

Icarus starts pulling to the left. Down the gravel road up the hill. Now that I think of it, I have never been up this path. I follow.

I can't believe I am beginning, again. All that progress for nothing. I feel like I had dreams, but now I can't remember a single one. I know that I wanted to see Montevideo since I was a kid. I guess I could do a trip. This last job did help my savings and my credit has been getting better.

But that's just avoiding the issue. I need a job. The world is on fire and I am a fireman. Maybe just give it a week. You were literally laid off this morning. No need to rush into something. Taking time to figure out what you want, can't hurt. Your mom will be patient, in that way that is impatient to try and get you out. Your dad doesn't respect free loaders nor does he care for hand outs. Fuck.

The trailer homes don't look too bad from here. I wonder why the front gets so dirty while the back remains untapped. You'd think it's the other way around.

How are we supposed to begin again when we don't understand the ending?

"You don't care for any of this do you, boy? As long as you got your meals, some sunshine, and some company. I wish I lived so simply. I envy you, Icarus."

In that instant a brown lab with blue eyes and a checkered bandana came trotting in our direction. Cutting through the tall beige grass. I pause my music and prepare myself. He looks friendly, but best I get big. I grip Icarus's leash.

A skinny kid with a mohawk came running in my direction. He has a red tank top and brown pants. He is barefoot, shouting his dogs name.

The lab just wants to play and Icarus is engaged. I let go of the leash, to let them bounce around for a minute. The kid catches up, grabbing the lab by the collar.

"Thanks, mista. He always be gettin out."

His shirt had the silhouette of Donald Trump with the phrase, *Onward to Victory.* Hasta La Victoria Siempre. I was teleported to my college dorm room in New York. I know I just failed my exam, but all I care about is reading The Motorcycle Diaries. I can't imagine Che Guevera and Trump would get along, but stranger things have happened.

Icarus took a mushy shit. Not a concerning mushy, but one worth acknowledging the texture of. We should keep an eye out. He is getting older.

As we walked back I was somewhat thoughtless. The sun was beginning to slip behind the mountain range. It's kinda strange that the sun isn't out for the same amount of time everywhere, but everyday only has twenty four hours. Actually that still makes sense. I wonder how long the sun is out in Costa Rica. Or Ecuador. What does a sunset look like in the Amazon? I tried to imagine it as I stared at the same mountain range I had seen for the last nine years. No matter how many images I tried to conjur within my mind's eyes, the only thing my imagination could produce is…silence.

When we got back to our house, I caught myself listening to the cars passing by beyond the line of trees. There was a pile of gravel next to the incomplete foundation. Icarus was sitting on the driveway very patiently. He swatted me with his paw.

"You'd want me to be happy, right boy?"

He swatted me again and began to smile. When we went inside, my mother was hovering over the stove.

"Will you be eating with us?"

"Do you mind if I eat in my room? Still working shit out."

"He might, but you know I won't. Just let me know how I can help. I am so sorry, my love. They didn't deserve you either way."

That definitely wasn't the case, but it made me feel good that she thought that.

"How was your walk?"

"Yah, no, it uhh, it helped."

"Good. I am glad, my love."

"Where is he?"

"You know him, he got an *idea* for a new rocking chair. He is in the workshop. Why don't you go help him? You both used to love that."

"Maybe later, mom. Call me when dinner is ready."

"Okay. I love you."

"Love you."

I ran into my room. Icarus followed. He tried jumping on to my bed, but needed a little boost. I sat at my desk and opened up my laptop. I stared at my camera on the shelf. I have been meaning to take more photos. As soon as everything got online, I searched "Used motorcycles for sale".

Embracing the Darkness

We were both searching. He read Paulo Coehlo and I read Dostoyevsky. He thought that made us the same. I thought it made us different. He had a unique way of viewing the world and once you learned how to speak his language it was quite…romantic.

He'd aways try my recommendations. No matter how strange, he always attempted. But nothing he ever presented me made me dive in. I felt guilty but I am very loyal to what I like.

I am not saying it's not toxic, it's just some shit.

He finally convinced me to do this thing in Brooklyn. A sensory deprivation tank. Get into water that is the same temperature as your body. Has enough salt to keep you floating. The room is as dark as it can get. You can choose music or no music.

You are naked, existing physically but all of your senses are—off. You are just the other thing. Whatever that thing is. The mind. The spirit?

We are sitting in the lobby waiting to go in. He is telling me about the last time he did it. He saw an iguana crawling across the night sky.

I am listening to this story, with a certain skepticism any rational human might adopt in this type of scenario. A Brave New World was at the forefront of my mind. But I thought, why not? You did your search. You see no risk. You want out of your comfort zone.

A twinky young fellow with glasses and a blad spot showed us the way. He got into one room, and I got into the one next to it. There was this white pod (?). Like if a white ferrari had been converted into a giant egg filled with jelly. Not jelly, but dense water. It just feels jelly-like.

I strip down to nothing. Stare at this pod-egg-piece of technology and I contemplate. Naked. In the light. Do I step into darkness?

My right foot went first.

I had braised my ass crack too many times when wiping. It was slightly burned. It was like sitting on a hot coal with the salt water. If this is going to work you're going to have to really concentrate.

I chose no music and repeated the breathing exercises you learned in yoga. That one time. Okay maybe three times. I went a couple times a week. It helped. Once I got the message, though, I hung up the phone. I am not sure what that says about me.

It was undeniably relaxing in the pod. The only thing was time was difficult to track. I couldn't tell if it had been three minutes or we were coming up on the hour mark.

I got slightly nauseous. I reach down for footing. I push myself off the floor and my head comes close to the ceiling. The shadows on the ceiling…comes closer to me.

You shoot back down. It's pitch black but there is a silhoutte. Just a few shades darker. If it were possible.

It lowered even more. Extending it's arms out to you. You explode at it's touch. It hugged you. Then it melted into you. Like butter on warm toast.

An announcement whispered into the speaker that, "the hour will be up in three minutes. The lights will slowly begin to turn on.".

Why was I crying?

We showered. Dried ourselves and then in a journal for all the guests wrote down our experiences. My friend reported on nothing more than a comforting silence. I told him I didn't see anything. I wanted to get my own interpretation in before I let someone else see my vision.

Was it a dream? My body feels lighter than it did before. Am I just dreaming that I am walking out on to the street? Could the visuals from the jelly be that good? I am just being paranoid.

I rode the subway to grand central then got on the next available train. I didn't really listen to anything or pay attention to anything for that matter. I was just really deep inside my own head.

The sun was down as I walked to my building. I climbed the stairs and smelt her cooking from halfway up the flight. The oblivion I felt in my heart, was temporarily masked by the aroma of a warm meal.

She had her headphones in, pijama bottoms on, and my shirt. She was more listening to The Sopranos then watching, as she hovered over the stove. Moving the frying pan around.

I kiss her on the cheek and thank for dinner.

"You have no idea. I got so much accomplished. Love having you around, but when it's just me—shit is getting done. You see those plants? Replotted. You see our books? Alphabetized! The plants told me something fascinating."

"Yah what did they say?"

"Those who want respect, give respect.", she squinted her eyes making a face like a jaboni (?). We laughed.

We are sitting across from each other, taking our time with our meals. Best to take a picture as an indirect sign of…appreciation (?). It works. She smiles.

We were both visibility tired. Not much talking happened as we just sat together. Occasionally smiling at one another. Grabbing hands. Feeling the glance of a flutter.

As I began to wash the dishes, she poured us a glass of wine each. She stood by, placing my glass on the counter, as I applied soap to the sponge.

"Why don't you use the gloves?"

"They don't fit."

"I don't like it."

"What you wanna sexier answer?", she nods her head gently as she presses her lips to the wine glass.

"I love the warm moisture all over my hands."

"Disgusting."

"You literally told me to."

"Yah but I wanted like Shakespeare sexy, not cheesy Ron Jeremy."

I pondered it over. She wants Shakespeare. I give her my heart day after day, and now she wants Shakespeare.

"You want me to recite something? I can look up something up that I like? Look up Sonnet 31. I remember liking it but I don't know the words."

"I'll look it up. You make up Shakespeare for me. You seem different, I can feel it. Make something up.". I stopped washing the dishes. I just let the warm water run down my wrists.

"There is something
That I must embrace
A loneliness of my world that
Lacks the color of your face.

It freezes me–
Trapped and terribly alone.
When my feet take the stairs,
To walk out this home.

The only thing that peels me
From my darkness
Is that my home tree
Occupies her brightness.".

She smiled. Looked down at her phone, and as I continued to wash the dishes, she read Sonnet 31. When she finished, she briefly mulled it over.

"I liked yours better. Fuck Shakespeare."

"Well, maybe not fuck Shakespeare, but I appreciate it."

"Yah, Shakespeare is pretty good."

"Half way decent."

We both laugh. Somewhere in the laughter, I found the silence of my shadow's embrace. I became distracted. I turned off the faucet and she suggested we finish our wine in the shower.

I was too tired. I hate to admit it, but I couldn't stop feeling this feeling. Like someone had snuck an envelope under my ribs. All I wanted to do was read it, but it was stuck inside of me. Instead of doing anything sexually, we just took turns washing one another's bodies. Sipping on our wine. Letting the warm water decompress us.

The blinds were down, so we sat on the couches naked and reading. I'd stop reading to jounral. She'd stop reading to change the song.

I poured a whiskey for myself. And got her another wine. She read an excerpt from her book that reminded her of my cousin. It took me a second, but I saw it.

I offered her a blanket and we threw some pillows on the ground. We laid on our carpet with our books in our hands. Soft guitar plucking playing like a whisper out of the speaker.

We both dozed off. But when we woke up a few hours later, we helped each other to the bed.

I was in a deep sleep. I was able to let go of the surreal memory and surrender to my exhaustion. When suddenly she woke in a panic. Grabbed my chest and gasped for air.

"Check the door. Check it now."

You jump out of bed and grab the umbrella behind your bedroom door. You turn your lights on and there is noone in your living room. You swing open the front door and look into the hallway. Of course, your neighbors are coming home and you are nude. You quickly shut the door. I hope they didn't see me.

I grab some water from the fridge. I go back into the bedroom looking down at the ground. "Everything alright? There was no—", her body is being pulled from the sternum by an invisible rope toward the sky. I quickly look in the mirror and see this dark matter consuming the doorway behind me. When I look back to my love, the same dark matter is pulling her in.

My glass slips from my hand. It shatters all over the floor. The displacement shakes me back into reality. She is sitting there with the comforter to her chest. Looking towards me with a screeching fear.

"There was nobody there. Sorry. I'll clean this up."

"Do it after, can you just come here?"

"What's going on?"

"I had a nightmare. A really intense one. I am sorry."

"Do you want to tell me about it?"

"I don't think so."

"It might help."

"I just don't want to freak you out."

"I am pretty sure the neighbors just saw my weiner. I posses no fear."

"Do not call it a weiner."

"Yes ma'am. My weiner and I are looking forward to listening to your dream."

"I hate you…I was dreaming that we were still laying on the carpet in the living room. Instead of waking up randomly, we wake up because there is a banging on the door. But like a serious banging. Like one of those knockers on old wooden doors in a medival village. Each bang the front door flexed like it was going to fold in half. We both stood up to hold the door. Then you told me to go into the other room. That this was your darkness knocking and it should be you that answers. I heard you scream from the living room and the bedroom door slammed shut. And all I kept thinking was I didn't tell you that I love you.".

She began to sob and fell into my arms. I told her I was okay, but I was not okay. I felt like I had transcended from this realm and that I now belonged to some cosmic darkness. I was frozen. Alienated within myself. And hopelessly alone. Everything around me was so full, but I was a vacuum.

She eventually fell back asleep. The street light from below gave the room a faint warmth. There is a tree by my window. The wind brushes it's branches against the siding. Occasionally, the tip of one scratches against the window like nails on a chalkboard.

It's been twenty six years. I have married, divorced, and remarried. Have a kid that adores me. Have another that can't stand me. I have seen some of life's wonders. Read some of the best books. Been honest when I can. And as I look out on the ocean of sand in the Sahara Desert. I find my shot on my camera. I wrote a poem about the desert's fatigue. This lingering silence of darkness that surrounds the candle of my dwindling heart.

If this is real, it's been well spent. If not then it has been a spectacular dream. But as I glimpse the universe from another angle, I cannot tell if this is all going on inside of me or outside of me. Did I ever leave the pod?

An Incognito Universe

Are you ready?, he touched his ear.

No, but it's the only play.

He passed me his cigarette as he exhaled. We stood side by side under an awning of a store front. The rain was really coming down. Across the street a truck was trying to squeeze between a car and the pillar for the overhead train. They took the rear light of the tesla it was parked behind. As it sped by the tires picked the rain up off the floor. As I inhaled, the mist raised within me.

There was a billboard screen. Viagra–fuck until your heart stops. Marijuana—be numb or be dumb! A cross, a buddha, and krishna were all sitting on a cloud with light pushing through–Listen to the calls and pick a contact name!

Now?, he touched his ear.

All there is.

Down the alley. Pop the cuff of my coat. Snuggle into my shell. He knocks on the door underneath the stairs. Once–three–once–twice. A man with a voice like sleeping thunder slides open the window.

"What do you need to say?"

"Monica Lewinsky was paid off by Jeffery Epstein."

He opened the door. It was a narrow hallway. An even bigger man with colliflower ear was sitting by the elevator. The walls were lined with mirrors. Across from him there was a small table with a painting under a lamp. I rubbed my chest. "Doubt is uncomfortable, Certainty is Absurd by Stefano Pallara." A replica in a small yellow frame. Log it.

He pressed the up button exactly three times, but the elevator will be going down. It opens; a blonde woman with white glasses and a red pony tail. She is armed with numchucks. He takes her right and I before her. We won't give her our back.

We won't give you our back. You understand., he touched his ear.

Invasion of privacy, accepted. I'd do the same., she wiped her brow.

The doors opened, music and lights poured in. I rubbed my chest. "Citizens Arrest–Dutch Hour Remix By NeuroBeatz, Dutch Hour. No reverse or foreign language detected. Proceed with caution." The lights seemed to have a limit in pattern. There were three people in pink latex two pieces. Two men and woman. They all had cobalt sparkling eye shadow. Various dangling earrings. Varying lipsticks. The first man pushed out a tray with small baggies containing a white powder.

If you want to dance all night., he touched his throat.

I rubbed my chest, "Pure Cocaine. You are in faze 10 best not to tamper with it.".

The woman in the middle had a necklace that read the word "Nobody".

If you want to fuck without taking your clothes off., she bit her lip and pushed the tray of pills forward.

I rub my chest, "Pure Ecstacy. We need you using your other head.". I touched my nose. She smiled. The third man showed the tray.

If you want your mind and body to have their own nights., he looked to the floor then touched his shoulder. Rubbed my chest, "Unknown substance. Very potent. Based off the chemicals seems as if it sends your consciousness into the cloud. Stay vigilant.".

The woman with the nunchucks walked past them. Her back to the dance floor she walked backward. Never taking those white glasses off of us. Until she pointed to the bar on her left; our right.

Wait there. I'll come when they are ready., she touched her brow.

We walked over to the bar. It's backdrop was a semi see through mirror. You could see the movement on the dance floor; the light bouncing. With the blue it looked like the movement of water in a storm at night. If you slowed it down you could see each molecule of a person transfer the vibration.

Old Fashion, I touched my nose.

Gin and tonic, he pulled his ear.

I held out my wrist and she dragged the knife through it. Very clean; precision.

I'll get his too, I touched my nose. She smiled and dragged the knife through again.

You have a good friend, she shut her left eyelid like laying a sheet on a bed.

The best, he touched his ear.

Our drinks rose from a hole in the bar. The bar had peach lights beneath white panels that had black mandala on them. The light shining through the design. I rubbed my chest, "Ingredients are accurate.". We clinked glasses.

Are you prepared for what happens next?, I touched my nose.

Difficult to say. Will you be okay?, he pulled his ear.

I was never even here. We must do what we must do, I touched my nose.

The song changed. I rubbed my chest, "Satan Was a Babyboomer by Brutalismus 3000. Translation seems safe.". I let my drink touch my lips three times, then put it down in two swigs. The burn felt off. Not the best old fashion I've had.

A black woman with red hair had numchucks in her belt. A red pony tail and white glasses; she approached us.

Come with me, she touched her nose. Then began walking backwards. Never taking her eyes off of us. She showed us to the door.

He tapped. Three–twice–twice–Three. A man with a voice like sleeping thunder slid open the window.

"What's your opinion of the Marvel Cinematic Universe?"

The ideal comic book movie would be a Daredevil movie directed by Stanley Kubrick, I touched my nose.

He slid open the door. There was an even bigger man with colliflower ear. He pressed the down button exactly five times, but we were going up. There was a small painting on top of a table with a lamp above it. How did they get Guernica into such a small frame.

When the elevator opened there was a small child with a katana. He had on a leather jacket and black sunglasses. We made the same pact. Neither of us would give the other their backs. He licked his lips.

When we arrived the walls and floors were lined with white marble. There was a man with a black grand piano playing slow jazz. There was a semi circle of couches. Everyone sitting on them was wearing black wool sweaters and black jeans. In the middle of the sweater was two crossed grey hammers.

"Come sit!", screamed a foreign voice. He waved us over with a hand that had a gold pinky ring. There were two seats available to the right of the matt. He took the seat closer to the guy standing on the wall. I took the seat closer to the boss.

"We don't use that other voice in here. There are some traditions worth holding on to."

Eastern European, potentially. We shook hands.

"You've been busy, Mr.Poet."

"I could say the same about you."

There were two gentleman wrestling in front of us. They wore a blue Gi that had the same hammer design on the back. They were black belts. They rolled in front of us and everyone had their eyes fixed on the men as we spoke. The only people not wearing the sweater were the man and the woman across from us. They were wrapped all over each other. Hoop earrings, silver teeth, clothes that dangled and was too tight. Alternating a tray of ecstasy that they delicately snort.

"We cannot deny the call any longer.", his eyes did not break from the wrestling before him. You could also tell in his eyes that he was listening to the piano with a great deal of attention. "The situation around the world is becoming worse by the day. After learning about the fiasco that was the last century the hope was that such violence was behind us. The truth is that all the horror–the rape, genocide, murder, and revolution are just as much a condition of humanity as love, passion, and intimacy. The violence is now unavoidable. You must understand this, Mr.Poet. What happens next is an act of compassion?"

"I am aware. Especially if there is fighting going on abroad. The situation here must be resolved quickly."

"Have you been drumming your drum?"

"As best as I could. Let's hope it is enough."

"Sometimes even the wrong train arrives in the right station."

We sat there and watched the gentleman wrestle for some time. He seemed comfortable. So did the boss.

"When these two are done and one is victorious", the boss points to the two who were snorting ecstasy, "We are going to watch them for a while.", she was feeling his thigh and he was caressing her neck.

"I think I'd rather just get it over with."

"Suit yourself, none of it matters either way."

"Agreed, but if you don't release them—then my people will come before you even see them."

"Don't underestimate us. We prepare for all contingencies. They will be released. The new world cannot be built on broken promises."

We got up. As I stood, I softly touched my nose. He understood clearly. Third shelf on the left; the key is in the vase; get to publishers as soon as possible. Sign out.

We shook hands. And as we made our way to the elevator, the boss shouted "You're doing a good thing!".

The elevator came with nobody inside. It took us down into a small room, again noone. We walked back into the club we were in previously. The music and the lights were blaring in the empty hall.

Not how I imagined it, I touched my nose.

I am proud of you, he pulled his ear.

I stepped into the room by myself. Rubbing my chest, "Feel The Rhythm by Fovos. Good luck."

As I got closer to the center the lights picked up. Transitioning from blue to purple to yellow–an explosion of beams dicing across me. In the center, I dropped to my knees. Looked up at the sky, touched my chest exactly two times. With exactly my two pointer fingers.

My drum stopped drumming. The body fell forward and when it hit the ground it pushed me out. The room had an eerie feeling of quiet, but the lights continued.

I was back inside the ether. It began to show me. All that I have feared. Crawling in from behind the corners. I sat down in the silent explosion of lights.

This is what change feels like.

I'd Rather Be Noone

"Guilty", was painted on the door when she arrived. Other doors in the building had the words "Guilty" or "Innocent" painted on the doors, but her's said "Guilty.". Assuming that this door belonged to her.

When we die, oddly enough we are given an ID card. This ID card doesn't say our names. The only information it provides is the age we died at. Down to the hours and minutes. Her's said "Twenty-six years, seven months, eleven days, five hours, thirteen minutes, and forty one seconds.". That was how long she lasted on earth. Or at least the Earth she had experienced since birth.

The other piece of information was to where she would stay. Her address, which would be difficult to find because this earth has no personal technology. At least not when you arrive. The ID itself, if you lay it flat on your palm, will slightly inch in the direction of your address. Therefore, all that is required is to follow the direction in which the ID moves.

She wouldn't know any of this. She didn't even know who she was. It was a miracle she remembered how to breathe and walk. Was it necessary to breathe on this earth? It's all unclear. All she knows is what the little girl told her in the park.

"I have been waiting for you.", said the little girl. She had pig tails. A checkered red and orange shirt with denim overalls.

"Where am I?"

"What is "I", may be a better question to ask, but maybe you might not like my answer."

"What is happening?"

"OOoooh! That's a funny question. Pinky promise you won't go crazy.", and she reached her pinky out to the woman. The woman clasped pinkies with the little girl.

"See people always believe they will know the difference. I remember my teacher, Miss Margret, used to say when we die that we would turn into a flower, or a cloud, Jacob was bad and she said if he keeps it up he'll turn into a toad. I member wanting to turn into a pink flower. But we don't really turn into anything. It's kinda like we turn out of something. Poopy! Father won't like that. Can you pretty please forget what I just said?"

"Sure. Do you know what's happening to me? Why can't I remember anything?", it was in this moment that she noticed an iron shackle clasped to her left wrist.

"I really didn't want to use the paper, but maybe I should. Sometimes my stomach feels like it has butterflies and other times it's like honey bees."

She looked at the little girl as she reached into the front pocket of her denim overalls. There were tall trees behind the girl. A row of benches and street vendors working. The trees arched overhead and the sky was was a blend of citrus with purple. She could see skyscrapers in the background. Distantly she could here the hussle and bustle of a busy street. Cars honking and chatter. She heard a saxophone and someone singing in the opposite direction. There was the clacking of a typewriter. There was a paved path before her, and when she followed the clacking with her eyes she saw on the bench before her was a man. Actually several men and women were walking in a stream of many currents before her, but across this stream was a man sitting on the bench writing on a typewriter. He had a sign that read, "Pick a Topic, Get a Poem". His hair and beard were long. He seemed happy. There were birds in the background.

"Okay. Otay! Listen, please. My father will be here soon, so we need to do this quick. What word is not for being able to wait?"

"Impatient?"

"Yuuhhh, that's my father. Take it with a grain of salt; he is a very busy person.", she looked at the girl with some confusion, but nothing really made sense so she accepted.

"I feel like I have been waiting five-ever! for you to come. I have missed you a lot."

"Do we know each other?"

"Perfect! That's where the paper starts. I'll start reading now, or maybe you should read? Some words are tricky."

"Just take your time and sound it out."

"Okay. Otay. Wel–come. I am you. You are me. I am also everyone here, in this new place. You are probably con–few–ed. We will give you some answers, but not all of them. This is the game of death. You can choose to play or not. We will tell you the con–see–kwen–seezes of both. Let us begin with what we cannot tell you. One, how you died.", the little girl began to count out on her fingers.

"Two, when you died. Three, who you are. Four, how long you will be here. These are the rules of the game. Now, I will tell you what you can know.", the little girl looked at her. Grabbed her pig tail and then shifted her body on the bench so she is facing her squarely.

"Do you understand?", she asked her.

"I think so.", the woman wasn't lying, but that doesn't mean she was not confused.

"Good. I will march forward.", she began to look at the paper again.

"You arrived at The InBetween via Central Park in New York City, New York, United States of America, Planet Earth.", she stopped looking at the paper and began to look at the woman directly. "My Father, likes to call it the InBetween here, but depending on the area this place is called many different things. My Favorite is when people call it The Arcade. Arcades are just so much fun."

"Anyways", she began to look at the paper again. "Why we arrive at certain places and not others is unclear. What we can tell you is that this was either the place where you died on earth or the place in your lifetime where you experienced the most happiness. You have a limited time here and that is one of the many things you need to find out if you would like to stay here. If you wanna stay here, you need to figure out who you were when you were alive. Then you can choose to be that person or turn to dust. If you don't figure out who you were before time runs out then you will just turn to dust."

"How much time do I have to figure it out?"

"Listen, lady! I can't tell you that."

"Do you have a frame of reference at least?"

"What is that?"

"What is what?"

"A frame of ref–urrr–wince."

"An idea for how long I have."

"Oh, no. Nobody does. Not even my father."

"Everyone I see is dead then?"

"Even the squirrels and the bushes."

"So, this is heaven?"

"Oh my gosh! I hate repeating. Please listen, lady! This is the InBetween. Heaven is so silly. You are either on earth, in the InBetween, or dust. Those are your options. Well, now that your dead only InBetween or dust."

"What happens after you turn to dust?"

"I don't know you are dust. What happens after you flick a booger?"

The woman began to scratch her chin. Why should she believe this little girl? For sure, she has no recollection of any past, but she does seem to have some basic forms of knowledge. She knows language and can identify objects in her surrounding, but if she saw her own reflection she would only see a stranger. What if she found out who she was and she realized that her thoughts were put into a foreign body? Nothing made sense at all. She had a sense of sense and reason, but no idea of identity. She has no conception of how she arrived on this park bench, either. She just sort of emerged. That's how far her memories go. She also could not shake this eerie feeling that something had just ended and something else had begun.

"You're thinking hard.", said the little girl.

"Well, you've given me a lot to think about."

"Do you believe me?"

"What other choice do I have?"

"It's funny that you keep using words like "I" and "me" when as of right now those things don't exist."

"How should I speak about myself then?"

"However, I don't care, I just think it is funny."

"You use the word, "I" and "me"."

"I do. But the rules are different when a kid dies."

"When do you stop being a kid?"

"I asked my father that once and he said it varies from person to person. Like there is no number."

"Do you know what the deciding factor is?"

"My father says, it's the moment you lose something about yourself in order to be yourself that you stop being a kid."

"What does that mean?"

"Lady, you do realize I am child? Nothing my father says really makes sense to me. I just know he is smart and I love him."

"So there are other children?"

"Sorta."

"What do you mean, sorta?"

She pointed at the guy who was writing poetry and then to the older gentleman playing the saxophone.

"Those guys never lost their memories when they came here, but they are older."

"Why is that?"

"They never lost it. Whatever it is. That doesn't mean they didn't face challenges, but they never let go of it. Whatever it is. There are plenty of other people like them. Some artists, some teachers, a lot of monks and priests, but most of them are in prison or cy–key–hattrick units."

"Interesting."

"My father is getting closer. If you have any more questions you better ask."

The woman thought things over. She concluded that she didn't want to turn to dust. She was just getting to know life again. Despite her limited time with it, she was clinging on to it with everything she had.

"How do I figure out who I was?"

"That's the right question to ask! There is an ID card in your pocket and it will lead you to a place that will be your home. The door will have your verdict. I can't tell you what that means either. But the card will show you how long you were alive for. Also if you lay it flat on your palm it will guide you to your home. You need to ask it to do that. Otherwise it will guide you to places that were important to you when you were alive. At your home there will be objects you were attached to when you were alive. Maybe there will be books, pictures, movies, paintings, or furniture. You can play with them and see if you can find clues. Or you can follow your ID card around and let it show you places. But what is really important is that you listen to your heart. You can do as much detective work and logical thinking as you'd like. It maybe will help, but the answer will be in the emotions. Whatever the clues make you feel will be what reveals who you were."

The woman looked around the park. She definitely felt at peace, but there was a buzzing ominously in the distance. The little girl looked at the woman and smiled.

"Yah you could tell you were a buzzer. You have always been one. When the buzzing gets louder that means you are getting closer to figuring out who you were and when it gets quieter you are really cold."

"What do you do when you have figured out who you were?"

"My father let me make this rule up! He can be so much fun sometimes. Basically on the other side of the door at your home there will be a piece of paper in a glass case. When you think you know, you take it out and write the poem that is in your heart. Once, you've signed it the poem is done and the game of death is complete. Depending on what you've written, the paper will either burst into flames or stay where it is. Oh my gosh! Here comes my father."

The little girl jumped from the bench and ran away from the woman. There was a stange man walking down the middle of the path. Nobody seemed to notice him. She jumped into his arms. The poet seemed to see this embrace and began to smile. He tussled her hair with a hand that was see through. The woman could not believe what she was seeing. Rather, what she was not seeing. There was a person in a black suit and a bowler hat. Where his face should be was clear and where his hands should be were also clear.

"Take a good look, lady! Once, you figure out who you are then you won't be able to see him at all!"

The two of them began to walk hand in hand down the path. Who was this person? As he walked past her, he lifted his sleeve to his head. Raised his bowler hat and the woman couldn't make it out, but she believes he tilted his head and smiled. As he put his hat back on, his cuff link fell to the ground.

"Wait, you dropped something!", the woman shouted.

"My father does everything on purpose!", the little girl shouted back.

"Please wait! I have so many questions still! Why do I know you?"

The man stopped and turned in her direction. He had no eyes, but she felt as though they were making eye contact. In the deepest recesses of her psyche an idea was communicated: *Does the seed know the flower? Can the flower remember the seed? Hold* onto your past or learn to be free? Is it the flower? Is it the soil? Is the seed? Are they one in the same? How tall would we grow, if there was no rain for trees? The two kept walking when the girl suddenly turned around and she was crying.

"I have missed you! Please, figure out who you are soon and come find me."

"When will I turn to dust?!"

"It could be in five minutes or two hundred years! Nobody will ever know!"

They walked away leaving the woman in contemplation beneath the orange and violet sky. She knew she knew the girl. She knew she was dead. She knew she didn't want to turn to dust. She wanted to act; what to do next? But she felt no motivation to do anything. At the thought of her lack of motivation, she felt the buzzing grow louder. Is that something about herself? She was not a motivated person? The buzzing grew even louder. Something about the buzzing made her slightly nauseous, but she felt as though she had just gotten her first piece of information.

"Here you go.", said the poet. He had just finished packing his typewriter into his backpack. He was now standing before her with a red leather journal. Holding it out to her.

"Do you need a pen too?"

"Yes, please. Thank you."

"It can be confusing at first, but it will get better with time. Writing down what you figure out will help."

The woman held the book in her left hand and the cufflink in her right. The cufflink was white gold and either had an "O" or just a circle engraved in it.

"They don't want you to know this, but they can't fully block your memories. At least, not without some help. That's what the handcuff is for. My opinion and it shouldn't matter, but go out and figure out who you are. Follow your emotions and all that jazz. But if you get that handcuff off then you will remember everything. Now, that's music, baby."

The woman stared at her wrist. There was a little key hole. The narrow end of the cufflink fit perfectly and she jambled it for a little, but to no prevail.

"You'll get it.", the poet said laughing.

"Why are you helping me?"

"We've all got different faces, but we are one in the same, baby. You've got the right to listen to whatever music touches you, but in the end it's all just music."

"Who are you?"

"Nobody. Who are you?"

"...nobody."

"That's the spirit!", he laughed and walked away.

She stayed on that bench for a while. Messing with the cufflink and the handcuff. Stopping, just to listen to the saxophone. She felt like it was getting late, but it wasn't getting darker. Do you sleep when you are dead? That would have been a good question to ask. Do you get hungry when you are dead? Why didn't she think of that when they were here?

She took the ID card out of her pocket. Twenty-six years, seven months, eleven days, five hours, thirteen minutes, and forty one seconds. Not a long time to be alive, but not a short amount of time either. She laid the ID flat on her palm, and it lifted while bouncing toward her. Home was me? She shook her head then turned around. There was a whole city behind her.

She got up from her park bench and began her way out of Central Park. When she arrived at sixty ninth street, she was crossing the street with her gaze completely fixed on the ID card jumping forward. She heard a honk and a truck was flying in her direction. She braced for impact, shut her eyes, and clenched her teeth. The truck just passed through her. She patted down her body; she was perfectly in tact and continued walking in the direction of the ID card.

She walked several blocks. Along the way she would stare at the glass windows of store fronts trying to see her reflection, but it was never there. Finally, an older woman told her that you can only see yourself in the reflection of your home mirror. She opened her notebook and wrote the third thing down:

1. I am not a motivated person.
2. It's all just music.
3. You can only see yourself at home.

When she arrived at the building there was a bookstore across the street. At the sight of it, the buzzing grew increasingly loud. She stepped into the street, toward the little shop, but it was as if the buzzing put her insides in a blender. She dropped down to her knees. She was convinced that she was going to throw up. A woman who looked like she was in her forties saw this and helped her up. When the woman got back onto the sidewalk the nausea subsided. After composing herself, she wrote down:

4.   Books (?)

The other woman who had helped her back onto the sidewalk grabbed her chin and lifted her gaze to her own.

"Are you okay, sweetie?", at the word "Sweetie" the buzzing returned in our protagonist. She quickly began to write down in the journal.

5.   "Sweetie" / endearment ?

"Yes, fine. Just a bit confused."

"How long ago did you arrive?"

"I haven't seen a clock or something. It's unclear. My guess is today. Does it ever get dark?"

"No, night doesn't exist in The Arcade, but you will get sleepy and hungry. Following your emotions is serious work. Have you seen your verdict yet?"

"I was heading there now. Do you know what it will mean?"

"The door will either say, guilty or innocent, but nobody is quite certain. There are certainly theories, but I can't tell you."

"Why is that?"

"I'll turn to dust if I get it right."

"How do these theories spread?"

"Well, for starters many of histories greatest artists, thinkers, and writers live in this world. Being in the after life has certainly given them much to work with. They come up with theories but encrypt the message. Conveying their ideas indirectly and in hidden messages because if someone interprets the right answer than it's not on them. But if they tell someone directly and they are right, poof, dust."

"Have you ever seen someone turn to dust?"

"Yes, one time a man and I became intimate. Finding love after death is a pretty spectacular thing and that's what he said."

"That turned him to dust?"

"Well, what he said was, 'Finding love after death has to be the purpose of this all–" and poof the woman dissapeared! Like a balloon popping, but instead of rubber flying in all directions, glittery specs rose toward the tangerine and magenta sky. The woman covered her mouth and screamed in horror. She fell to the floor and staired at the spot on the sidewalk where the woman once stood. After a moment she opened her notebook, but fearing that she may turn to dust for repeating the words she took the advice of the great dead thinkers. She was cryptic in what she wrote.

   6. Find a rose in a garden of cemetery weeds.

Those words were enough to remind her of what the woman had said just before she turned to dust. She felt herself growing tired. At the recognition that she was tired the buzzing returned. She thought this was strange, but wrote down her seventh clue.

   7. I was exhausted.

The woman entered the building with her back to the bookstore. There was a concierge who looked at her, squinted, and said "Two thousand and seventy sixth floor.". The woman couldn't remember how tall buildings were when she was alive, but this felt alarming. She got in the elevator and had to type the floor number into a monitor.

Considering how high she needed to ascend the ride felt relatively short. She definitely had a moment to review her notes and reflect on the conversation with the little girl. A man made of glass was her father? Why'd he give me his cufflink? She took it out of her pocket and began to jingle jamble it in the keyhole. It seemed to fit perfectly. The doors opened and the handcuff showed no indication of coming off.

She stepped out into an empty hallway. The walls were beige and the floors were carpeted brown. The doors were a stange blend of the two colors. The word "innocent" was painted in red on some doors. The word "guilty" was painted in a navy blue on other doors.

The ID card took her left then about as far down the hallway as she could. All the way at the end in the right corner, the ID turned in that direction. "Guilty". She looked at it for some time. An instant of denial came over her, but before she could turn away from the door, the ID card jumped from her hands. Plastering itself above the word.

The door behind her opened up. In a coarse and tired voice, one like hot honey being poured over gravel, a man spoke, "Don't overthink. It's just a fucking word. The whole lot overthinks it, but there is no thought to it. A game of random to fuck with us lowly folk.". She turned and faced him.

His face was round but sorrowful. His white hair with brown-black roots was receding and slicked back. He wore a white striped short sleeve button down, with khaki pants. In his right hand was a whiskey neat with a burning black and mild between his fingers. In his left hand was a copy of "Chung Tzu" and "The Bell Jar" by Sylvia Plath. His eyes were blood shot.

"The name is Charlie. Most just call me…actually I don't remember what people called me.", she looked at his door across the hall from her and it said "innocent".

"Easy to say with the word, innocent, painted on your door."

"I can see it in your eyes. You've got spit, kid. Suppose by that bracelet, you don't know who in the shit you are."

"Just arrived."

"Well, I'll tell you that you're a writer, or at the least an artist of some kind."

"What makes you say that?"

"All true creatives are idealists. That's why it hurts so damn bad. That's also why they put us all so high up. We got our heads in the clouds type of thing. If there is a designer of this place, their a sick fuck. Real poetic and comedic bastard."

She took out the red notebook and wrote down:

8. Creative.

"The beatnick in the park gave you that?"

"You know him?"

"Yah, we are gonna meet up at this jazz spot downtown right now. Normally, I don't leave the place too often. There are just a few more things I wanna read before I turn myself to dust. My wife couldn't figure out who she was in time and it hasn't been the same without her. You can knock on my door whenever."

"I appreciate that."

"The roaches and rats in my spot might not agree with you, so I'll bring the bourbon to you."

She laughed at the sight of this miserable old man. Not at him. With him. He chuckled a dry chuckle as well.

"Nothing could cure the loneliness of an old man like a pretty young thing such as yourself. You know they say you can't get pregant in The InBetween. Nothing quite excites me like a challenge and I have chopped down bigger trees.". The woman's compulsion was to slap this dirty old man, but she found herself blushing.

"Umm, offer appreciated?...I think I am gonna try and figure out who I am first."

"A nice toe curler will tell you a lot about yourself.", he smiled as he took a drag. On the exhale he began walking down the hallway and laughing.

She shook her head, but couldn't deny the old man. Sex had to be part of who you were.

9. Try to orgasm.

She took a deep breath and walked into the apartment. Hard wood floors. Cadet grey walls with tall ceilings. A grey couch pressed against the wall. Three farm house windows that were almost as tall as the walls. They were in a wood farmhouse style. They revealed a view of a small backyard with a garden. The grass was very green and freshly watered. There was a round table with three chairs. A hammock tied between two trees.

A classical tibetan rug in the center. It's border was crimson with the internal being a mandala of various blues. The center was also a crimson lotus. The borders of the mandala's design were also crimson.

There was a five story bookshelf with a writing desk next to it. The shelf was filled with a variety of female writers. Sappho, Ayn Rand, Dorris Lessing, Bell Hooks, Agatha Cristie, Simon De Bevoir, Angela Davis, Octavia Butler, and Virginia Woolf to name a few.

She opened up the red journal and underlined number four. And then put a parenthesis next to it, writing down "Female Writers". From the moment she walked into the home she felt a low frequency buzzing, but there was certain things that she would look at that made her unbearably nauseous. These were clues that were difficult to engage with.

She felt an inclination toward each book on the shelf, but if her approach was to read them in hopes that they would reveal something about herself, then she needed to begin where the buzzing was the loudest.

There were three books written by a woman named Elizabeth Cane. *Under the bluest moon* was the first. *In a fiery sky* was the second. *Toes in the grass* completed the trilogy. She felt an attachment to these three works of fiction, but the buzzing was unbearable. She knew it was were she needed to begin and yet…

Her finger grazed the top of *Under the bluest moon* and her uterus jumped to her throat. Her throat dropped to her rectum. Her thoughts were submerged. Her heart was on fire. She sprinted to the bathroom. She intuitively knew which door it was behind. Lifted the toilet seat and began to throw up.

The buzzing increased. She thought, "I am sick." and the buzzing confirmed the observation. With puke still on the corners of her lips, she rested her back against the wall. Her head resting on the white tiles next to the toilet paper dispenser. She wrote down another clue.

10. I am sick.

She unrolled some toilet paper to clean her face and chin. Slowly standing up to confirm her legs were beneath her; she flushed the toilet. Turned on the faucet to let cool water run on her wrists, then splashing some on her face. There was a navy towel on the rack by the mirror. She went to grab it, but there was a face looking back at her. The corner of her eye caught itself in the reflection. With water still dripping down her jaw she slowly turned her gaze. The buzzing became so loud that it transitioned into a silent absolution.

Before her was a face. Her face. She finally recognized herself. In front of her was an observation of mahogany straight hair parted in the middle. Naturally straight down to the shoulders. A nose with a calm bridge. The same height of it's peak. She smiled at the sight of herself. Revealing vertical tip lines that so badly wanted dimples to compliment her round cheek bones. Cheek bones she followed up into her dark brown eyes. The shape of the eyes were slightly slanted but overall large and round. Like they were eletrectured with the sight of life.

Oddly enough, taped to the mirror was a paper mustache perfecty aligned with her shorter stature. When she stood perfectly in the center, the paper mustache fell between the reflection's nose and her plush upper lip. It was black and pointed upwards at the corners.

She stared at the mustached version of herself and giggled. With water still dripping from her face she opened her red notebook. She had new clues but found it difficult to come up with the words to describe them. After a few minutes it came to her.

11. I am me.
12. An odd sense of humor.
13. I am beautiful.

She dried her face and looked at the reflection once more. She couldn't really make out her ethnicity. She felt like she could be Russian, but no buzzing. Italian? Still silent. Turkish? Nothing. Greek? A low frequency.

14. Part Greek.

The buzzing got louder when she wrote the words down. Mexican? Again, nothing. Venezuelan? Nada. Korean? Not even close. She was closer before she thought. Argentinian? Perfecto. The buzzing came in nice and clear.

15. Part Argentinian.

When turning to leave she saw a teal stepping stool tucked into the corner. The natural light in the room wasn't bad, but she wanted a better look. She flicked on the lights and slid the stool over with her right foot. Propping herself up on it, pressing her palm on to the counter, and leaning in really close. She is inches from the mirror. Staring deeply at the details of each brown pupil. All the fragments and explosions. Then deep into the black abyss of the pupil. Trying her absolute best to see if there was someone in there.

No buzz; just darkness. Darkness and a profound conviction of something. But what that something was eluded her consciousness.

16. I believe in something bigger than myself.

She left the bathroom having learned so much in very little time. She went into the bedroom and their were photos framed. The buzzing was low as she looked at each one. It was always her with another person, but the faces of the other people were all scratched out. In the corner were two yellow canaries in a white cage. She could tell they were the quiet kind. As she looked at them she knew they were both female. That one was older than the other. The buzzing came in and she opened her notebook.

17. Mother and daughter.

Her comforter was a soft white and the mattress was soft to the touch. She jumped into the bed. The pillows were feathered; her head sunk into them. The buzzing returned.

18. Gentle comfort.

She saw the door to the closet. When she opened it there was a lot of denim and neutral colors. A box dedicated to sunglasses. To the right of the box was the head of a mannequin. Wrapped around the neck was a silver necklace. The pendant was a waxing crescent. It's borders were the same silver while the inside was a smooth jade. She touched it and felt safer. She immediately put it on. There was a buzzing, but she was unsure what to write down. She just left this clue alone. The necklace wasn't going anywhere.

When coming out of the closet, she realized the bed was elevated off the floor. She peared under to see tubs. At the sight of the tubs the buzzing turned into a violent screaming. Quick to attention, the silence rushed over her in chilling goose bumps. A similar feeling to the books by Elizabeth Cane. Her back pressed to the wall—she felt a vertigo jumping and thought she might throw up again.

With wobbly legs she made her way to the bed; sitting on it's edge. There was a night stand to her left with a lamp on top of it. There was an arabic tapestry designed into the lamp shade. It was an image of a story. There were a group of men trying to pull their animals across a gorging river. She flicked it on and the light shined through on the outlines of the animals, the men, and the rushing current.

She slid open the first drawer where there was a black notebook. A hell fire whistle buzz came over her. She slammed it shut. In the rush of silence that overcame her she threw up a little in her mouth. She swallowed it. She collapsed into the soft pillows once more.

What should she do? She gently rubbed the jade moon. Staring at the ceiling no thoughts and no buzzing came to her. She turned to her left and stared at the canaries in the cage until she slipped into a gentle sleep.

When she woke up she continued her search in the living room. Then made her way into the kitchen where she made herself some breakfast. To her amazement when she placed something, like her milk, back into the fridge and shut the door, it would be completely restocked when she would go back. She quickly concluded that she had an endless supply of groceries in this kitchen. She decided to eat outside in the sunny backyard. She sat at the table and came up with a plan of action.

She had concluded a few things since her arrival. Had come up with even more clues to lead to eventual conclusions. Some of those conclusions were as follows: She was dead. She didn't want to turn to dust. She was afraid of herself. She believed in herself. The trilogy by Elizabeth Cane, the tubs under the mattress, and the notebook in the nightstand contained her truth.

As she sat the table she could hear birds chirping and her canaries replying. Since the canaries are here, are they dead too? To be dead and trapped felt too cruel. Though she enjoyed the presence of the birds she felt a certain duty. She went back inside into the bedroom grabbed the cage and came back out. She opened the cage door but the birds remained inside. She hung it on a branch of the tree with the door open.

As she sat there having her coffee, she knew that she preferred three sugars and light cream, and eating her breakfast she watched the dangling cage. The canaries just sang their song— perched with their wings glued to their sides.

She concluded by watching the sway of the cage that perhaps the buzzing was a muscle. Or a tolerance to the buzzing was like a muscle. Without a doubt the trilogy, the tubs under the bed, and the black notebook had the answers she was looking for. It was logical considering the fact that time was of the essence to begin her search into herself there, but she couldn't even look at them without being nauseated to the point of almost throwing up.

She thought if she began with more tolerable clues and built her way up to the real answers then perhaps she will be strong enough to handle them. She had to come up with a system.

When breakfast was done, she sat at the table for a while. Again, staring at the swaying cage with it's door open. She reached into her pocket and began to jamble it into the handcuff. After some time, her results were disheartning so she went back inside.

She removed all the books from the shelf. She went through each one thoroughly. Beginning with the books with the lowest buzzing, she began to return them on to the shelf. Placing the one with the faintest buzz in the upper left corner. Each book placed to the right of it had a slightly stronger buzz. She did this until the top row was filled. Then the second. The third. The fourth row. Finally, the fifth. The last three books in the bottom right corner being, Under the bluest moon, In a Fiery Sky, and the last book on the shelf Toes in the Grass. Even moving these books around made the woman feel like she was going to faint.

She thought for the sake of being thorough she should begin at the beginning as opposed to wherever she felt comfortable. She believed this was definitely a risk, but that seemed intuitively worth taking. She grabbed the first book in the upper left corner. Went back outside and laid down in the hammock. She read it all the way through. Writing down clues in her notebook and ideas in the margins. Whenever a scene would stump her she would just stare at the canaries cage overhead. Door opened, birds singing, and choosing to remind trapped.

When she finally finished the story she felt filled with ideas. She wanted to keep her thoughts organized and didn't feel comfortable exploring in her red notebook. She went back through the apartment and knocked on Charlie's door. He answered with a stumble.

"I was just thinking my coffee needed some sugar."

"Very sweet, Charlie. Listen I need a favor to ask."

"Ah, so you decided to take me up on my offer."

"Not quite. I am working stuff out over here. I haven't quite made time for your suggestion, but from what I can tell that activity isn't the most important in my life. I was wondering if you had any paper."

"What kinda paper?"

"Any kind. I just want to write and a lot."

Charlie went back into his apartment and left the door cracked. The woman was able to see into the apartment. Everything was an army green and there was cot in the middle of the room. On top of it was a single pillow and a lime colored wool blanket. Beneath the cot were scattered books, empty bottles, and an ash tray. From where she stood it didn't seem like there was any other furniture.

"Here you go miss lady.", he handed her two reems of printer paper.

"This is perfect. Thank you so much, Charlie."

"Don't sweat it, kid. When you gonna have me over for a meal?"

"When I have got some time. I have come up with a system and I think I'll figure out who I am soon, but I need to hurry."

"Ah, so you're the practical type. I'll be hearing from ya."

He shut the door and she wrote down her newest clue.

33. The practical type.

She went back outside and sat at the round white table where she had breakfast. The birds were still in the cage. The sky was amber and lavender. She remembered the words of the woman who turned to dust before her. If she gets it right, then she too will turn to dust. She decided to be cryptic. To express her ideas in a narrative as opposed to an informational style. The book she read created two conflicting emotions in her. One of the emotions felt feminine, whatever that means. The other felt masculine, whatever that means.

She created two very basic characters. One man and one woman. Each character identifying with their respective emotion. She then locked them in a room with no windows and no furniture. It became less of a story, but more a series of monologues. When it finally concluded she felt like she was beginning to grasp something, but something didn't quite fit.

Grabbing a fresh sheet of paper she began again. This time she gave the female character the attributes of the masculine emotion, whatever that means. She then gave the male character the attribute of the feminine emotion, whatever that means. Again, the story and the conflict was expressed through a series of monolugues, but this time the story ended in a passionate sex scene. A sex scene that felt very natural to write and revealed a great deal about the nature of the author's desires.

She opened her red notebook to write down a series of clues that were revealed through expressing in this way. Before she knew it she had almost fifty clues into who she was. She now felt very confident in the system she developed. She felt if she was loyal to it, then in no time she'd be able to engage with the hard truths. The woman agreed to attempt engaging with the trilogy, the tubs under the bed, and the notebook every five books she completed. Getting closer each time, hopefully.

Though this system was exploratory, well thought out, and revealing it was undeniably taxing. By the time she was done with her two stories our author was exhausted. She dragged her feet into the bed room and collapsed on to the bed.

When she finally woke up she repeated the cycle. She would repeat the cycle indefinitely. She attempted to engage with the three hard facts after her fifth book and seventh story written, but to no prevail. Everyday she would wake up, have breakfast, watch the birds with their cage door open, read a book, write a story, uncover clues, and dedicate some time to shoving, twisting, and turning the cufflink into the handcuff. Always unsuccessfully.

By the time she finished the first shelf, a longer narrative began to brew in her head and develop in her heart. She was beginning to realize that when she was writing the buzzing would cease. But not in a way that revealed she was going against her nature. Rather, she was so aligned with her nature that the only natural result possible was such a deep immersion into the buzzing that the only thing truly revealed was a serendipitous silence.

For fourteen sleeps, she skipped reading and would write until exhaustion. By the time she had used her imagination to create a whole world, filled with conflict, tension, and an unsatisfactory solution. She would spend an additional three sleeps rereading what she had written and writing clues about what the plot revealed about her.

Then it was on to the second book shelf. She continued the process of reading an entire book and then making up stories as a reaction. Every five books she would get closer to revealing one of the difficult truths. Well, to say getting closer is a bit generous. The progress was there but it was minisuclue in comparison to how much she was learning about herself by staying loyal to her process.

Again, when she got to the end of the row the birds remained in their cage and she had another long narrative brewing in her head. She repeated the process of diligently working through fourteen sleeps. Then three days of reviewing what she wrote and coming up with clues. When this process was done she realized she was running low on paper.

She knocked on Charlie's door again. When he answered he was in a stained shirt and had no pants on. Just boxers and midcalf socks. He was visibly drunk. Again, he attempted to sleep with our inquirer and again she turned him down. She explained her situation, there after he went inside to grab more paper for her. He left the door ajar and before her laid the landscape that she had sworn to memory. The only difference was above the cot rested a very large abstract painting.

The borders were a mustard yellow and as you followed the colors toward the ceneter it bended into a warm pink. Until finally a blank square where no paint had touched it. The square seemed to be suspended by streaks of violent paint splattered. From the border of the untouched square to the borders of mustard yellow were streaks of neon blue, deep purple, and subtle orange. Sort of presenting itself as a suspension system of webs holding up the blank square. A blank square in the center with a single black brush stroke in it's center. Our woman stared at it and felt a distant buzzing that she could not identify with any certainty.

"Here ya go, my love.", Charlie said as he handed her the reems of paper. This time it was three bundles. He followed her gaze into his own apartment and onto the painting above his cot.

"You like it?"

"Like what?"

"The painting. I made it a while back. You inspired it. Would you like to know what it is called?"

"I don't think so. I'd rather not know, I mean. It's pretty…pretty stunning."

"You can have it if you think it will help."

"Really?"

"Really. I like making art, but holding on to my own work feels pretentious. Maybe this will warm you up to the idea of keeping this old man warm at night."

He walked back inside and plucked it off the wall. Carried it by his side and walked it over to her door that still read, "Guilty".

She thanked him as he brought it inside her apartment. He nailed a nail above the couch and hung the painting. She offered him a glass of water or wine and he said he wanted to leave her to her work. He did take a solid peak around the place.

"Very revealing", he said.

"What do you see?", she replied curiously.

"You, obviously."

There was a pause in the room. She looked around the apartment with the new painting on the wall. She concluded that she too saw herself in the small place. As Charlie was leaving he decided to share one final piece of information.

"If you give this old man a kiss, then I will tell you your name?"

"How do you know my name?"

"Been spending more time outside. You were quite famous on Earth and your popularity is growing quickly in the InBetween. You should get out more. You may learn a thing or two."

She looked at him suspiciously. Then curiously. She figured she was already dead. She laid her lips on his. He tasted like cheap whiskey and smoke. The old man grabbed her ass then fondled her breast. She liked the way it felt, but she pulled away and slapped him clean across the face. He licked his lip that was now bleeding.

"Dead or alive, being slapped by beautiful woman has a strange euphoria to it."

She felt that she shared in the euphoria of slapping him. She composed herself, "What is my name?"

"Elizabeth Cane. But from what I have read your friends call you Beth."

The buzzing made her stumble back a few steps until she finally collapsed onto the couch. The painting suspended over head. She looked at Charlie dangerously.

"You were a talented writer when you were alive. Your stories and your death impacted a lot of people."

She could feel it. He was telling the truth. She had already had some suspicions, but remained in denial about the notion of her talent. Charlie grabbed the door.

"Next time we speak, I am coming for more than a kiss and a slap. Though I am open to them being included."

He left and as the door shut, Beth accepted that she too wanted to fuck the old man. She looked forward to running out of paper, again. She opened her notebook and wrote down some more clues.

376. I am a writer. I was a famous one too.

377. My name is Elizabeth Cane.

378. My friends called me Beth.

379. Under the bluest moon, In a fiery sky, and Toes in the Grass were all written by me.

She sat on the couch for a while staring at the piece of paper attached to the door. Could she write the poem now. Did she know enough about herself to capture the verses of her heart? What would happen to her if she got it wrong? She sat there debating for a while. It was too difficult to tell. She also had this deep feeling that she had more time to spare. There was no evidence to this claim, it was just a feeling. She went over to the books shelf and tried to grab one of the books she had written. To no prevail the buzzing was just immense beyond control.

She grabbed the first book on the shelf. She went outside to her hammock and got to work. When she finished it, instead of writing, she grabbed the next book on the shelf. Back out to her hammock. She was tampering with her system. Instead of writing after every book and testing one of the difficult truths every five she decided to make a change. She would write after every five books. Test herself after every twelve.

Her writing undeniably became more complex and layered, but the real reason she was doing this was she wanted to make the pages last as long as possible. She was avoiding seeing Charlie, again. She knew what would happen when they met again. She couldn't deny it. She hated that she was attracted to his roughish nature.

380. Men are disgusting, but I like to fuck.

She also found herself staring at the painting whenever she thought of him. She couldn't make out what it revealed about her, but she knew it revealed something.

Eventually, she made her way through the third shelf, the fourth, and finally the fifth. Stopping of course when it came to her own novels. She also couldn't touch the tubs under the bed or the black notebook in the nightstand.

What was she to do now? She had exhausted her system. She knew some aspects of herself but not enough to feel confident writing the poem and signing her name. She sat on the couch beneath the painting while shoving the cufflink into the handcuff. Again, with no luck.

That's when she remembered something Charlie said. That everyone on this floor are idealists. To be an idealist is to seek the ideal of something. She was a seeker. Maybe if she could answer the question of what she was seeking, then she wouldn't need to have face her truths. She decided she was going to go out into the world and ask her ID card to show her what she wanted. Before she did that though, she wanted to understand the nature of her pleasure.

She knocked on Charlie's door. A woman answered.

"Hello", the woman said politely. Beth was shocked.

"Umm, hi, uh, hello, greetings. Is Charlie here?"

"Is my name Charlie? I don't feel any ringing."

"No, no, um, did you arrive recently?"

"It's hard to say, but I think so. All of a sudden I was at a museum staring at a painting. It was called 'Christina's World'. Anyways there was this piggish old man. He made many sex jokes. He had a whiskey and a thin cigar with him. I couldn't remember anything. I still don't. Anyways, he told me I was dead and that I had to figure out who I was. He was giving me many instructions and then he said his father was coming. All of a sudden an invisible man appeared in a suit and a black hat. They walked away together. I just followed my ID here."

"Did someone give you a notebook?"

"No, were they supposed to."

Beth reached into her pocket and grabbed her red notebook. When she opened it all the pages were blank. Besides the very first line. In an unfamiliar handwriting it said, "Hand it to her if you want to know the truth about yourself. It begins with generosity.". Beth shook her head, but then offered it to her strange new neighbor.

"Writing down clues will help. It was confusing for me at first, but it gets better. Also it sounds like you met Charlie. Out of curiosity, what was the last thing he said to you?"

"Um, he turned around as he was walking toward the stairs. He just shouted, 'Tell her I'll miss her.'".

Beth smiled. She looked at Beth with concerned eyes. "I am really scared."

"Don't be.", Beth replied calmly, "Just play the game. You have got a second chance here. Make it last. You may even find love after death. Wouldn't that be nice?"

"It would be. Can I ask you something else?"

"Yes, but I've gotta run so make it quick."

"Why does my door say 'Innocent' and yours say 'Guilty'?".

Beth looked at doors and began to laugh uncontrollably. She then looked at the scared new comer.

"The designer of this place has a sick sense of humor. It doesnt mean shit."

Elizabeth Cane began walking towards the elevator without looking back. If she still had her notebook she would have written down one more.

381. I hate regret.

She thought about Charlie and the painting he made as the elevator descended into The Arcade. The concierge smiled at her as she exited the building. She stared at the bookstore. It's unclear how long she looked at it, but the buzzing she was experiencing was now tolerable. The woman working the counter saw her through the window, pointed at her and waved. The embarrassment was too much for Beth. She turned her back to the woman, pulled out her ID, and asked it to show her everything she had ever wanted.

It began to hop to the left and she followed. When she got to the cross walk there was the little girl with pig tails across the street. They made eye contact and like the day in the park she heard a voice in the deepest depths of herself. It was the girls voice: "Don't forget to look up.". The girl vanquished in the blur of rushing cars.

Elizabeth took the advice to heart. She drank in the city. The skyscrapers, the rushing cars, the rushing people, the street art, the street performers, the chaos, and the music it all created. All while fixing her peripheral on the hoping ID card.

Finally the ID brought her into Grand Central Terminal. It began floating as she stood next to the ticket booth. The buzzing came in like water pressure pushing through a small crack. Then she looked up at the celestial mural. Instead of looking up at the night sky she felt as though she was looking in the direction of the earth from the opposite side of the universe. A conductor came up to her, handed her a ticket, and said "Track 36."

The ID fell back into her hand and she made her way to the track. She boarded. Her ID showed her into a window seat. It departed. It was the Hudson Line. As the train traveled north, the ID pressed itself onto the window. Elizabeth didn't break her stare. She was filled with the same sensation she had when she would write. She decided to shove the cufflink into the handcuff. The sky was a fiery saffron blended like watercolors into a vibrant mauve pink.

She messed with it for some time. Elizabeth was startled as she felt a novel traction. She looked away from the river landscape and down at the handcuff. She began to twist towards the right and almost lost the progress she had made. She quickly twisted to the left. There was an undeniable click. The handcuff opened up.

If her mind was a stream, it was now a running river. If her soul was a trickle, it was now a ferocious waterfall. If her heart was a gentle fountain, it was now a violent gorge.

The train stopped, they had arrived at the Ossining station. "Please stand clear of the closing doors.", came over the loudspeaker in a robotic voice. She looked down at her wrist. Where the handcuff had been opened revealed a cut that was wide open. Her eyes watered as she stared at it. As the doors to the train began to shut—she clicked the handcuff back on. A silent buzzing. It all disipated and she was heading nowhere, again.

The Boy With A Coiled Tail

It's weird because she is here now, but I still don't know her. I miss my room. The couch is soft. Lucy curls into a purr as she sleeps under my chin. The cars driving by at night always shine a light in through the blinds. The shapes of the shadows make it hard to sleep.

Not in like a bad way. Well, not always in a good way. Sometimes the shapes make me think of something and then I see a movie in my head. I just don't like it when it's a scary movie. Like that time my older brother showed me Disturbia. I hate when I see bad things in my head. The next morning I am so tired and distracted. Do you think there is something wrong with me too? My brother is studying to be an engineer.

Today, is birthday number 12. I can't remember any birthdays before eight. My dad says this is normal. I have seen him eat a tuna melt sandwich while driving. I don't know if he knows what normal means. I don't know if I know what normal means.

Anyways, it's just me, mom, dad, and grandma. My mom's mom. They tried to convince her to move to the United States when the war started to get bad. My dad said that she used to just say, "I've made a deal. I will be okay. Everything will pass.".

When I look at my brother in the eyes I see a bridge. When I look my mom in the eyes I see cotton candy in the sky. When I look my dad in the eyes I see that big rock by the lake. When I look at grandma Amela in the eyes...I don't know. It just goes on forever. It makes me feel the same way looking at the shapes at night makes me feel. Not always good.

It's like the movie begins, but the whole thing is black with red music. I think she knows I am scared of her. I actually think she thinks it's funny. Whenever I look at her, right before I run away, she smiles. Her skin has so many wrinkles and her teeth make me think of that wooden stair I helped my dad replace last summer. It was the wrong type of wood for the porch. The rain really messed it up. My dad let me keep it, he didn't know why. He said, "Normal kids don't like to play with rotting wood.". What does he know about being normal? The wood was hard and soft at the same time. It made me think a lot.

This morning I woke up really early. There was a bird by the window that made Lucy angry. After I woke up my lips felt like licorice and my tongue was like a pork chop.

I went into the kitchen and Grandma Amela was standing in front of the window. The sun was rising. She was facing it with her hands on her chest. I slowly poured my self a glass of water. I sipped it slowly as I watched her. Her wrinkles looked different in that morning light. She finally looked toward me.

"Vater me tew. Berry gewd four jew."

She walked over to me. Kneeled down so she looked me directly in the eyes. The movie of shadows began to play. She grabbed my cheeks with dry hands and angular fingers.

"No fear. Eye see jew berry many tyme. Love. It have fear. Dis jew kill like da bull. Gloria in power. See me. See bird. See you. See world. Jew see. No fear. Love."

I don't really remember the rest of my day. I know the storm got bad, so nobody could make it to my party. My dad said, "being disappointed is a normal part of life. It happens.". What does he know about normal?

Grandma Amela was really in the clouds. My dad would ask her questions and she just stared at her dinner plate.

After dinner my brother facetimed my mom. We talked for a really long time. He is the smartest person ever. He knows so many things. I hope when I get older I know things. All I really know now is that I don't know a lot.

He told me that he was learning how to use a computer design program to generate blueprints to be printed by the schools 3D printer. He asked if I remembered that bridge he designed in his senior year of high school. I didn't remember everything but I can never forget how hard someone works. Everyday after for school for hours at his desk.

He said it would change the way we looked at overcoming problems forever. The idea was perfection. There was this time in High School when he showed me what he was working on:

"Santi, what you need to understand is all ideas are perfection. It's when we try to bring them out that they become imperfect. This bridge design is perfection."

"Marco?"

"What's up bud?"

"If it's perfect because it's ideas and ideas get messed up when you try to bring them out, then how will you not mess up your idea?"

"I won't try. I'll just bring it out."

"You work on it everyday. Isn't that trying?"

He thought about it for a while. His eyes fixed on the ceiling. He did that and would twist his wrist like he was turning things over whenever he was thinking really hard. Marco is so cool.

"Working on something everyday doesn't mean you are trying; it means you are devoted. I am consistent but the work is effortless. It is really natural. It's like I am breathing. Do you try to breathe?"

"No."

"That's how you do it then. The perfect idea becomes the perfect thing by effortlessly breathing life into it."

"Marco?"

"What's up bud?"

"Do you think I can be an engineer too?"

"Is that what you want?"

"Maybe."

"Can I tell you something?"

"Mhmm."

"I really liked that short movie you made on Dad's phone."

"That was silly."

"It had a message and it made me think. Was it hard to make?"

"It just sorta happened."

"So, maybe start there. Watch some YouTube videos about filmmaking and some good movies. See what happens. If it doesn't feel effortless, then engineering isn't going anywhere."

It was nice to talk to Marco on the phone. It made me not care that noonce could come. We couldn't stop laughing because he grew out his mustache. He told me he had a girlfriend now. That the next time he visited would be in two weeks for Thanksgiving and she was gonna come with him. He was excited to introduce, "his favorite person to his second favorite person.". I didn't know which I was, so I decided to hate her.

My grandma looked at me at this moment. She smiled with those hard/soft teeth. Then she dragged her finger across her throat. Then used her fingers to give herself horns. She smiled. Did that happen or are the movies in my head getting better? This old lady makes no freakin sense. She started laughing to herself. Then she got up and grabbed as many plates as she could carry.

When I hung up with Marco, I went into the kitchen and Granma Amela wasn't there. I went back to the living room and told my parents she was missing. "Old people wandering off is comepletely normal.", my dad said. What does he know about being normal?

"Check upstairs. I want her to see you open your gifts. She traveled all this way.", my mom said. She has been quiet ever since grandma Amela got here.

I looked out the window and saw a strange cloud developing. It made me think of this book Marco showed me. About a fisherman in the sky. His boat road on clouds and his hook would catch finches. He lived at a lighthouse and prayed everyday. It had really cool pictures. I wanted to see if I could find it on his shelf.

When I walked into the room all the lights were off and some candles were lit. They were all placed in a circle. There was a design in chalk on the wood floors. In the center of the design was a red candle, a red leather book, and Grandma Amela. She was naked. Just from the light of the candles I could tell there were wrinkles everywhere.

She had one fist pressed to her forehead and the other was pressed to her chest. Everything in me said run, but the movie of shadows made me freeze. She was whispering something. Then she looked at me and waved me into the room.

"Come. Kill fear togetha. Love iz oogly sometyme."

Lighting struck outside and the room was smacked in white for a blink. I began to move effortlessly. I bet my dad doesn't know Granma Amela has tattoos. What does he know about normal?

It Began As A Mistake

The last time I was driving down an open road, with no intention of ever coming back, was seventeen years ago. I ended up returnng back then. I won't now. Neither time did I inform people on my plans to abandon society. I just abandoned them. I remember when I was somewhere in Virigina my grandmother called me. She told me that dinner was going to get cold. It was 2:17 AM at night.

"What do you mean?"

"You were just in my dream", she told me very slowly. Years of screaming at children and grandchildren, along with bickering at her husband that she loved to hate, had withered her voice. She is a tremendous tree that sounds like a fallen branch.

"You were just in my dream. I looked out my window and you were cutting wood with a red axe. You'll never believe this but Maria

Callas walked into my room. She told me to call you because your dinner was getting cold."

"I just had a cup of coffee, Yaya. I am okay."

"Are you lost?", I think about this question a lot.

The inclination to respond to such a question with, "Who the fuck isn't?", is so compelling. So extremely compelling one might even describe it as a compulsion. One feels compelled to act? Feels a compulsion to act?

Compelling is like your friend is drowning. His hand breaks the surface of the water. You see this palm and you know it is attached to someone. Not just someone, but someone you love. Well, we don't love all our friends. At the very least the hand is attached to a person who is associated with memories that are pleasant. Actually, some of my best friends. When you really get down to the knitty griddy, the hand is attached to a person who is associated with memories. Do people with alzheimers have friends? Or is friendship entirely contingent on memories? Maybe I don't know. You would feel *compelled* to offer them a hand. If you are a decent person they won't even need to ask for help. You would just help them. Compelling emotions aren't always the morally correct action.

Let's imagine the person wants to drown. From some sort of a moral perspective you think because you offered your hand a person is alive. That must be better than the opposite. That would be a correct assumption. Maybe I am not sure.

Let's suppose the drowning person wanted that for themselves. Is disobeying someone's personal wishes for the sake of their well being ever justifiable? In this scenario most likely. Would it make a difference if the person drowning was a criminal? What about the type of crime? Shop lifting versuses rape?

I am getting lost in the details. What I think, maybe I don't know, is that the compelling emotions creates a very unique scenario. In some sense it is like action that is compelled can be seen as spontaneous moral judgments through decision.

Compulsion is like you are the one trying to drown yourself. You didn't plan it through so you don't have a lot of things making it easy. No rocks in your pockets or anchors attached to your laces.

Everything begins to tighten up and in an instant, maybe I am not sure, that you were trying to hold yourself down—you have broken through the surface. The distinction is vague but there definitely feels like one.

Being compelled to behave is spontaneous moral judgments through action. Compulsion. Compulsion…Compulsion?

If the hand reaching out was attached to a criminal, maybe I am not sure, but a real heinous criminal. Like such a terrible criminal and horrible person, that they are the republican primary and a very serious candidate for the presidency. You may be compelled to reach out, but you could stop yourself.

Could you stop yourself if you were experiencing a compulsion? Is that the distinction? The degree of agency in acting compared to not acting. If that is the case then, maybe I don't know, I should redefine what it means to be compelled.

Because in defining spontaneity, it feels implied that a condition of spontaneity is lack of control. Maybe I am not sure. I think, behavior of unknown origin might be better, but there is a characteristic of control. Or lack there of it. To engage with the unknown you must relinquish what you know. So, how can what distinguishes compulsion from compelling be the degree of agency in compelling behavior versus the lack of it in compulsive. Especially when I consider the fact that in the defining of compelling behavior it is implied that there is an element of releasing agency. I am back where I started. A different atomic make up of blacktop beneath my rubber tires.

I am moving so things are different. The road is still open. The sun hasn't risen. Seventeen years ago I was in a similar circumstance.

"Lost in the sense of never having been here before, but not in the sense of not knowing where I am heading.", I said. Have we ever been where we are at? Ever? Do we ever know where we are heading? Ever?

Maybe I don't know.

"Why don't you come home? Whatever it is we can get through it. Together. As a family."

"I can't."

"Why not?"

"I promised myself to go somewhere I have never been, Yaya."

My Yaya raised me. My mom worked two jobs and my dad…

Now that I think about I don't know what my dad did all day. His hands were always clean, but I remember him being a mechanic. Maybe I don't know.

She would give me tasks to do after school. If I was good she would reward me with McDonalds. In the car ride over she would go through a variety of Greek albums.

"If you cannot see your culture, then you must feel your culture.", she would say as a mantra. Recited each time the first track loaded.

I liked the songs. Maybe I don't know. They were good, it's not what my friends were listening to though.

At her funeral two years ago I talked about these blessings she used to do. I never understood the words (she always said them in Greek and I never learned), but she would always say that if the blessing worked you'll know because you will yawn. The yawn is a release of an evil spirit.

I made a joke that she would always give me these blessings late at night or after a day of play.

After the ceremony, my son approached me. He gave me such a big hug. It was the first time I had seen him since I lost custody. His mother had been using the alimony to pay for guitar lessons to try and win him over.

"I wrote a new song on my guitar. I think you will like it a lot."

"What about the lyrics? Are you still writing poetry?"

I have nothing against music or musicians. I just wanted my son to be a writer like his old man. This is a lie. I wanted him to be a better writer. The writer I could have been if I had his resources.

"Not as much. This might sound silly but I feel like my story telling has really came into itself through chords. I am still telling stories just…differently than before."

"I am happy for you, lil possum. Just remember good songs require great lyrics."

In terms of valuing art by qualitative standards, music is undeniably the most sensual medium. It's the only art form that demands presence. Are you compelled to be present? Is your presence a compulsion? Damn. Is there even a difference? Maybe I don't know.

Why you gravitate to whatever medium you do is beyond me. I have this feeling we are trying to recreate something from our childhood that we don't even know we remember. Maybe I am not sure. What I do know is….

"Have you talked to mom?"

"When I can. She wants contact to a minimum for now."

"She thinks she can just get me things and pay for classes. I want to be with you. Nothing is going to change that."

"I want to be with you too, lil possum. But sometimes the truth is more important than our desires. The truth is I shouldn't be around anyone. I am a real mess."

"I don't care. I love you. You're my dad. You're my friend."

What do I know? Ah! That with time you begin to become your medium. Become a musician; be sensuality. Nothing wrong with that, but to embody paraxodes is the mark of a good human. Writing is nothing but a paradox. In it's conception it is one. Using ideas associated with specific sounds to identify objects, people, and places. Then taking the sounds condensing them even further into symbols organized in a horizontal fashion. Organizing the symbols so their sounds correlate with some sort of abstraction. It is a ridiculous practice and yet when it is successful there is nothing quite like it.

"You don't get it. I hurt the people I love. I need space to work things out. Just listen to your mother."

"What about Pablo Neruda?"

"What about him?"

"I am supposed to read him by myself?"

"For now. Poetry is for either for crowds or quiet rooms and whispering."

As you become more skilled at writing the virtues of the craft rub off on you ten fold. Good writing consists of being informative and engaging. At points, fun and at others sad. At it's best it is simple and complex. These are all characteristics of strong independent people. So even if you're not famous it's a medium that benefits you. I am not successful and I write regularly. It hurts sometimes. Does it ever hurt too much? Sometimes, maybe, I don't know.

My gradmother continued, "I understand. Just listen to me my love. Going where you have never been is how we find ourselves. I discovered that much when I came here with your grandfather, God rest his spirit. Just know even though I found a home away from home, I still go back and visit. I hope you find what you are looking for."

"I hope so too, Yaya."

"Do you own a blue axe?"

"No."

"See if you can buy one if you go camping. That's my guess. You always loved the outdoors."

"I have my tent with me.", I was heading towards a campground in North Carolina.

"Trust your dreams just as much as you trust your intuition, my love."

"I will, Yaya."

She hung up the phone. My dinner is getting cold...

Seventeen years later I am heading for the same campgrounds. People and places change. Nature does too. Something feels different though about the passage of seasons– death and rebirth–compared to a new building being constructed along your favorite walking path–death and rebirth.

When I arrived at the National Park, it had an uneven dirt road. It was March. I thought it would have been colder. It was mainly overcast and had been raining since I drove into the state.

I found the first open lot. It had a charging stand near the parking spot. Society has infiltrated nature. If the woods had Wifi I would have thrown up.

Once I had pitched my tent, I sat at the picnic table and opened my laptop. My plan was to write until I had absolutely nothing left to say. This was going to take time. I gave my self a hot spot and began emailing realtors. I was beyond caring for the judgment of others so I was very transparent about my abandoning the world. That nothing existed that could convince me that the irrationality of this decision made it a bad one.

"I have a digital copy of my deed. The post office isn't far from the campsite. Let's get my house on the market as soon as possible."

With the funds I had in my account I could stay out here for a few years. It was twenty dollars a day to camp on the lot. I need an additional couple hundred a month for grocery runs and fire wood.

I brought every canned food I could find. I even stopped at a grocery store to clear out shelves. The blue axe that I bought seventeen years ago came along. It took me sometime to find it but I did. My initials were carved into the handle with a pocket knife.

I also brought with me every book in my library that I had not read. A total of 739 books. I am compelled to buy books often? I have a compulsion for buying books? Maybe I don't know.

The plan had very few rules. I came up with them on my road trip over.

The first, I cannot leave the campground until I have eaten through all my supplies. The morning of my arrival I made eight trips to various locations. Buying all the firewood and lighters they had. I also bought a tarp to cover the wood.

In less than a day I had enough supplies to last me a year and a half. For this year and a half besides the occasional meal with a stranger, my diet consisted of a can of beans in the morning. A can of corn for dinner. I didn't have a scale with me, but the little clothes I brought didn't fit the way it did.

The second condition, I wouldn't write a word until I finished reading all the books. I wanted my imagination to be so richly marinated that each word written was a declaration of pleasure. Pleasure of the highest degree. The words mascerating pleasure as they conceal the suffering of belief. Believing in yourself when nobody else does is a tenuous enterprise. But it is of noble pursuit. Before it can be good for others, it must be perfect for me. Maybe I don't know.

The books are loaded in boxes in the truck. Stacked in many tubs. I'd wake up with the rising sun. Get the fire going right away.

Throw the can of beans on as soon as the flames are tall. Put the coffee grinds in the press. Put it over the fire. Do some push-ups, squats, and run a few laps around the campgrounds. Once I get back from my run the beans are hot and coffee is ready to blow.

I sit beneath a tree.

Just listening. It is silent, but it's nature's silence. Birds are flying by. Just high enough so I can make out there silhouette through squinted eye. There is a ghostly exhale whispering as I watch. I can make out the wind as it wraps around the wing of the shadow bird.

A dove flew at me once. I thought it was a dove, but when it got closer it turns out it was a crow.

Maybe I am not sure.

Then I'd have my can of beans and my coffee, after having given them a half an hour to cool off. It was getting warmer by the day and so warm coffee only began to agree with me in the chilliness of the evening.

Then I'd grab a book from the tub. Set up the hammock and a chair. With the book in hand I'd walk around the campsite reading. Bouncing between positions as I saw fit. One time I roamed into the woods while reading. It took me a long time to find my way back.

It was because I got lost that I began my practice of walking. See once I began a book I wouldn't stop reading it until it was done. Only taking breaks to eat and use the bathroom. It needed to be one time all the way through. Or as close to that experience as possible.

The only problem with this strategy was when I would begin the next book I'd sometimes be distracted. Then I remembered how clearly I was thinking when I was making my way back to the campsite. So I started walking.

Whenever I finished one of the books—it didn't matter what hour of the day it was—I'd start walking. I wouldn't stop until I made peace with whatever I had just read.

The tubs contained the wide range of my interests. From astrophysics to literature. From psychology to history. From journalism to botany. Religion and encyclopedias of nature. There was a really fascinating book on birds.

There were random travel books from all over NY. Did you know the town Ossining. The one that has the prison. The name has it's origins in a Native American language. Derived from the term sint sinkt, meaning stone on top of stone.

It's a miracle the way a book can make you realize you are still grieving something you thought you had moved on from. That's not the only thing they do. They make claims about the world. Sometimes by it's various functions and facets, but mainly on perspective. The infinite ways the world can be viewed and understood is a virtue highlighted through the arts.

That perspective always shines light on an aspect of my identity. I am now forced to engage with whatever it brought up. I walk to let go of whatever it has brought up in me. To find my way to strength, in order to let go of it. Some books bolster my ego others break me to nothing.

I never know. I just grab what I can and read. If I am between two, I follow my curiosity. This was the routine of my life for quite some time. It was very fruitful.

Enough cans of corns and beans inevitably lead to some harsh bowel movements. Like tryna push plato through a straw. I drove into town and bought a hundred dollars worth of stool softeners and laxatives.

At the checkout was a woman with silver hair. It had a balayage of purple streaks. She looked at my dirty fingers that held numerous bottles of bowel relief.

"You're at the campground down the road?"

"Yah. How'd you know?"

"I smelled you before I saw you. Also, I live on the grounds too. I am the host. I checked you in when you first arrived. I live in a trailer that has a kitchen, a bed, and a shower. Though, I don't have as many books as you do.". Now that she mentioned it she did look familiar. Only then she wore sunglasses and a long coat. Now she wore a tank top and blue jeans. It was like those blue jeans were fitted to her strong legs.

Her left arm had a tattoo of a phoenix. It was red ink. The style was like brushstrokes of water color.

"How do you know about my books?"

"You're not the only one who roams the grounds. What's up with your ass?"

"My diet has made it difficult to go."

"What's your diet?"

"Cans of corn and beans. Coffee and water."

"Jesus…how about this? I'll come by tomorrow with eggs and bacon in exchange for a book."

"Deal."

The next morning she came by and I asked her why she only had one plate. She didn't know what I meant. I told her my assumption was that we would have breakfast together. She walked back over to her trailer, while I ate my breakfast. By the time she got back with hers, my plate was empty.

"I thought we were eating together! To believe that I thought I was in the presence of a gentleman."

I pleaded for her forgiveness as I poured her a cup of coffee into a spoon silver mug. It just had been so long since I had real food. The anticipation got the better of me.

"Tell me a story. In exchange for your forgiveness."

A story? Yes. A story. Tell me a made up one, something from your books, or one from your real life. I had just finished reading a book on poisonous frogs. The image of the golden poison dart frog was seared in my mind. There is this frog, I said.

It is sometimes known as posion dart frog or golden poison arrow frog. Eukaryokta. Animalia. Cordata. Amphibia. It has these dark marble eyes. The feet on the hine legs sometimes come past the elbow. The skin is this inviting yellow. I couldn't stop thinking about how if I saw it the color would obviously serve it's purpose. I'd know not to touch it. But at the same time something about it's color makes you wanna get close to it. I found myself inches away from it's image in my book. Anyways, I love this little frog. It's lethal in an adorable way. Like this little cute thing is one of the most poisonous species on the planet. It looks like an adorable key chain. Oh, they are indigenous to Colombia.

She laughed. We spoke about our lives. How we arrived here. Why we gave up on the outside world. Before we knew it we were breaking into midday. She said she needed to check the bathrooms and organzie payments. As she walked away, she turned and asked how I liked the sunsets by the bay.

"Haven't seen one yet."

"Really!?"

"Mhhmmm."

She looked up at the sky. Like she was looking for something. She found it and redirected her gaze my way.

"I'll meet you by the water before the sun goes down."

"Thank you for breakfast!", and she walked away.

I was reading The Narrow Road to the Deep North by Matsu Basho. The last page or two I was wondering why the acorns at this park are so hard and sharp. Actually quite large. And literally everywhere. The trees are tall and thin. The grass is green blue. Once the sun begins to dim in that evening sky, an owl–somewhere near by—begins hooing. There is a rhythm to it if you pay attention.

I hear the hooing and think, it must be time to go see the sunset.

By the time I get there Kaitlyn is waiting for me. She is just resting on the railing. Looking out on the water.

"Let's walk the path. By the time we do a lap the sky will be changing."

I followed her lead. I wasn't familiar with the path. It was narrow. Tall thin trees arching over to the right and the left. Eventually the brush of trees ended at an beam bridge. It was in the center of the beam bridge where you could see the marsh below. The bridge's throughout the wetlands connected small islands of thin trees. When I looked to my right I could see four other bridges in the distance. In between one of them was a sandhill crane. It's presence was brightened by it's surrounding beige tall grass. The water was also clear but very dark.

To the left was the opening of the bay we had just seen from the dock. Just from another angle. You could see a road in the distance. A bridge connecting the gap that begins where we are standing. Spreading outward like a V. Until the ends of the letter open up into the distant Atlantic Ocean.

I looked out, hoping my son was okay. I must have hurt him deeply, but I would've done worse damage if I stook around.

Sometimes compassion looks like a moment of pain for a lifetime of joy.

Kaitlyn and I kept walking. Bouncing from small island to small island. Continuing to get to know each other. I told her about this book I read where the main character kept choosing to be alone. He did it so much that he eventually turned into a coyote.

She asked me if I believed in God. I told her I don't believe in anything.

"Anything?"

"Besides the fact that people are better off without me in their lives."

She seemed dissapointed, but also understood this statement.

It was with that one comment where I became aware of the fact that Kaitlyn was romantically interested in me. Maybe I am not sure.

Eventually we arrived at the bench at the end of the path. The top left plank was snapped. It was on a sandy bank. We are looking out on the creek from the bay. Across the creek is tall thin trees and a few old strong ones. At the top of one of the strong ones, there was a perched bald eagle. We both sat on the bench and watched it in silence. The water moved from left to right. Back home it moved from right to left.

I got a tattoo of a smiley face on my pointer finger many years ago. Kaitlyn noticed it and held my hand. She told me it was a silly tattoo. That she preferred silly tattoos to serious ones. She then rolled up her sleeve and showed me a tattoo of a pineapple.

"I watched a lot of SpongeBob when my kid was growing up. Plus they are delicious."

I found out she was the same age as my grandmother when I first came down here seventeen years ago.

We began walking back. She told me that I was the first guy to not assume that her trailer and truck were her husbands. It seemed obvious to me that she was her own.

She smiled at this comment. Kaitlyn was in fact romantically interested in me. My abandoning society had broken the barrier that restrained desire. I found myself becoming aroused on the walk.

What would her silver and purple hair look like as it draped over her breast?

We arrived back at the pier. The sun was beginning to slip away to the right of the horizon. As I looked out on the sky a crane came gliding down to the water. It grazed it's claw upon the surface of the water. Leaving a streak upon the once still bay. It settled into a brush of tall grass.

The color in the sky came to life. I have never seen such warmth. I am drinking it in as best as I could. Then I look to my left and her eyes—

Everything in sight was suspended within her gaze. Her skin glowed. There was a youthfulness to her experience. She sees me looking and smiles.

"My favorite color is sunset.", she says. Immediately followed with, "Do you smoke weed?", as she pulls out a bag of prerolled joints.

She pulls it out placing one on her lip. Her lip…why is it as though I am seeing a lip for the first time? She sparked it. Exhaled and handed it to me.

I have not smoked since college but I couldn't even conceive of turning it down. Kaitlyn, this purple haired goddess of freedom, and the warmth of this setting sun has awoken something in me. A fire that I do not know how to extinguish. I took a drag. Exhaled. Looked at her converse. Looked out on the sea just beyond the bay. The crane was still. I took another drag. The wood on the railing was coarse. If I slid my finger faster I would have had a splinter. I exhale.

"Kaitlyn?"

"Yes.", she takes the joint from my hand and looked at me. I felt like I was the only person that ever existed.

"Can we fuck? I mean—can we make love? Uhm, do you wanna fuck me? Geez. Uhm, I think you're wonderful. You are single. I am single. And I can't stop looking at you."

She let out a loud laughter.

"You are very cute, but it's going to take more work than that.", she handed me the joint.

Books have given me a unique insight into the wolrd, but completely broken my romantic compass. We talked and laughed.

The sun began to set completely. On our walk back to the grounds I said a joke about how the guy in the lot at the part of the road that is like a horse shoe. That he looks like a cricket that forgot how to fly. At this point the weed had fully hit us and we began to laugh uncontrollably.

When we got to her trailer she kissed me and grabbed me through my pants.

"Come shower tomorrow morning and I'll make you breakfast in exchange for another story."

She went inside and I cut across the field toward my campsite listening to the hidden owl. It took some time to get the fire going. I threw the corn on and read Basho in the moonlight. I took down two laxatives. Just finishing the book I ran into the woods. When I came back I decided to lay down in my hammock. It was tied between two trees. I fell asleep under the stars.

In the morning I cut through the field with all its dew. When I knocked on her door she was still sleeping. She had chairs set up outside so I sat on one and began reading the copy of Leaves of Grass by Whitman I had grabbed from the tub.

Eventually she came out and her hair was wet. She was wearing a washed pink robe.

"There should be hot water still. I left a towel on the door. Clean yourself three times over if you have to. I never want to smell you, again. Your breakfast will be ready when you're done. Don't take long."

The campgrounds had showers but only cold water comes out. Maybe I am not sure. See I only showered once. So as far as my experience is concerned the showers only have cold water. But my pool of information is extremely shallow.

It was very nice to have hot water run all over my body. I found myself so deeply relaxed that I forgot to clean myself. The water began to turn cold and I violently spread soap throughout my body. I washed myself over and over. But no matter how much soap I applied the water was brown against the white floor. It was getting colder by the second.

Finally the water became clear and I smelled more soap then dirt. I got out and changed. When I came outside she had both plates waiting on the table. She was drinking her coffee with her legs crossed. Revealing her thigh through her robe.

"I actually waited for you."

"Much obliged", was that cool? Maybe I am not sure.

We ate together and then sipped our coffee in silence. I thanked her for the shower and breakfast. She cleared her throat.

"Here is the deal, kid. I am gonna take a risk. If you make me pay for that risk nobody will find your body. I have no clothes on underneath this robe. We are gonna go in there and we are going to have sex. Partially because I want to and partially because we have an obligation to the gods. I do not know who is in charge but our paths clashed and we know an exclusive kind of freedom. We owe it to the universe to have sex. It's how people like us play our part in keeping things in balance. No fucking me like I am virign, I need you performing like you have something to prove."

She wasn't asking. When she finished talking, she grabbed the plates and I grabbed the mugs. I followed her inside.

A few hours later I left the trailer lethargic. I was oozing in a post-cum fog. The sex was all over me. She had taught me so much in such little time.

The next time we saw the sunset together we laid out the ground rules. I told her about my ambitions. The mission I was on. She told me she valued nothing higher than her peace and her children. Our dynamic could never come between those things.

We both had become accustomed to solitude so not having it wasn't an option. We also didn't want to risk it becoming romantic. So we agreed to have sex in the mornings after breakfast and then go on with our days.

This put a certain structure to my days that wasn't previously there. I'd spend the late morning reading and by the early afternoon I needed to take a nap in my hammock. Then I'd wake up and keep the fire burning. I read so many things. Surely having sex was slowing me down a little bit, but it felt like it was worth it.

I lived like this for a while. On this cycle. My friendship with Kaitlyn became more intimate, but we never crossed boundaries. Our love making became more playful. At first it was a fiery passion.

Then it was a joyous exploration. The mountains brought moaning and the valleys brought laughter.

Eventually the seasons began to change. I remade my tent a little closer to a tree. I found a long stick. Dug a hole in the appropriate spot and placed the branch against the tree. The other end in the hole. Then with some water I packed in the dirt so it would stay in place. I had some rope and tied it to the tree. Underneath the branch was my tent.

I covered my tent in the tarp I was using to cover my depleting pile of wood. Then grabbed other branches and used the original branch to serve as a support beam. My tent had a roof. Then for a week I was collecting pine cones. The sharp and hard ones. I was pilling them up between the tent and the branches.

Eventually it was stuffed. It wasn't perfect but my tent was insulated. At the very least it would block the wind. I moved the fire pit to the foot of the entrance.

I survived the fall and the winter like this. After new years, Kaitlyn caved and let me sleep in her trailer with her. We barely slept. We went four days naked in her trailer as the wind blew against the window. During this time, I read the Cosmopolitanism and then the Bhagavad Gita. I watched her make eggs. Her long hair reaching down to her bare butt. Every line I read—this woman was evolving into something more.

She was a breath of divine. Atman proclaimed pleasure through her dharma field. Whatever that even means. We were united in every movement. Whether we were physically intertwined wasn't relevant. I felt the quiver of her heart. She knew when I was close by. Something had extended out us and the other embraced it wholly. It was such a small space and we navigated it like a dance. We were one. Oneness. This must be Allah. No, there is no god, but God. Perhaps it was all around. Yahweh? Or just experience. Perhaps it was the freedom. The part of it that brings pleasure.

"If I was forty years younger, I'd have your baby.". The comment caught me off guard.

Eventually the storm passed. We agreed it would be best if we went back to some solitude for a while. That I'd come by tomorrow morning.

I am not sure why, but I never went. I just stayed at my campsite and read. It was something by Noam Chomsky.

The next morning I woke up and thought it best that I go see Kaitlyn. Clear the air about why I didn't show up. When I arrived at her lot her trailer was gone. Everything was gone. My heart melted in heavy globs. I dropped to my knees. My vision screamed at the palms of my hands.

Eventually I made my way to the campsite. There was an envelope taped to the hood of my truck. "For Mr.Mystery" was written by a feminine marker. Inside was a letter:

"You're a bastard. A real rotten bastard. I told you I was taking a risk and you threw it in my face.

I wanted to tell you at breakfast. I got offered another position to be the host of a different campgrounds. Canyon Lands National Park. In Moab, Utah. That's where I am heading right now. I knew the second I saw you it would get too real too fast. I took the job.

You always insisted on me calling you Nobody that I never got your name. To think I fell in love with nobody and it was realer than any of the somebodies of my past.

I need to know I am not just a convenient way to pass the time. If you love me the way I love you. Come find me. "

I held it for a while. I thought maybe I can look her up on facebook. I grabbed my phone from the glove compartment. Turned it on. Before I could get to my Facebook app messages from everyone began to pour in. Everyone I left behind. My son was calling everyday.

I panicked and threw the phone as far as I could into the woods. I clenched the letter. I didn't know what to do. The only thing that helps me think is reading. I go to the tub to grab a book. It is empty. Yesterday's was the last one.

I lift the seat of the truck. Under neath are three leather journals. Each one is pretitled. One says, poetry. The other, novel. The third, philosophy. I got the fire going. I am going to have to restock for the third time this season soon.

Do I go after her? Or do I began to write now that I can? I can't decide. I sit by the fire and listen to the morning become evening.

My approach to the poetry is just to listen. Allow all the sentiment to pour out in words. However they come out.

The Novel is going to be about a man who has lost hope in the world. After getting caught in the rain he decides to sit beneath a tree in the park. Just to stay dry. When the storm passes he is grateful for the tree.

He stands and kisses the tree in the park of a busy city. The tree in exchange for the kiss grants him the sight. He sees the beginning and end of time. He is young but has many regrets. He discovers in his revelation that in your final moments of consciousness, you hear a song. The lyrics are written by the words you have said. The rhythm is based off the emotions you allowed yourself to feel.

Oddly enough this was also the song that you heard without realizing it when your consciousness first silently whispered itself into existence.

That was all I had in terms of plot. From there I suppose I'd have to make another character. Give them a personality. Create some sort of conflict and follow my intuition.

The philosophy notebook was going to be spent in a less academic style and more a meditative plea for the necessity of resisting conformity. That the truest way to have a relationship with any higher power is to get away from the structures imposed on you. And be the agent of meaning for your experiences.

I held the three notebooks by the fire but I could feel Kaitlyn's forearm in my hand. Mr.Mystery...

Who am I?

The question left me...

There were so many stories in my head and for what cost. My boy calls me everyday and I never answer. I have abandoned my child for an idle dream. Only to find love and run from it.

I sat by the fire all day, never once thinking about making corn. The next day I woke up and walked the path she had shown me. I sat on that bench all the way the end. There was no eagle this time. I did see a few cranes but the day was greyer.

By the time I got back there was a car parked at my campsite. An old Subaru Outback. The sun was starting to come out. The day was getting warmer. There was nobody inside. Just empty bags of chips and empty water bottles. A couple of energy drink cans.

There was nobody around so I just got the fire going. When the flames were really cracking a voice emerged from the woods. He had a tired hair style in a combover. A mustache. An ancor tattoo on his forearm.

"Who throws there cell phone into the woods. It took me forever to find it."

"Lil possum?"

"What's up, big possum?"

It was my son—he was bigger. He had a tattoo now. A mustache. He had changed. Of course he changed. That's what happens when time passes.

"You have a mustache.", I said as we hugged each other. I began to laugh in an emotional manner. He was tearing up.

"Very cool ink", I said, "When did this happen?"

"A couple months after high school. Your hair and beard…"

"I look cool right?"

"You look like Walt Whitman got bussy fucked by Osama Bin Laden."

"I am not sure what any of that means, but I did read Leaves of Grass. I regret not reading it earlier in my life. I tried to read it the first time I abandoned society."

"You mean this isn't the first time you do something like this?"

"That's not relevant. The real question is what are you doing here?"

"I have missed you a lot. Nobody understands me like you do. So I called and I'd check your location. Yesterday your location popped up. I didn't know what to do. I just started driving as fast as I could. The only thing I grabbed were a couple changes of clothes and my guitar."

"You don't go anywhere without your guitar do you?"

"Not really."

"You in a band?"

"I have musicians who come with me when I do gigs. But most of my stuff is solo work. Not an official band or anything. What I am trying to say is I have a band but no collaborators at the moment."

"You are doing gigs?", I showed him where to sit and I sat on the floor by the fire.

"Yah. People like my stuff. I am not a paid musician or anything, but it feels like I am on the right track."

"Right on, man.", we fist bumped.

"Can I get you something to eat? Your options are a can of corn or a can of beans."

"Uhhmmm what kinda beans?"

"Listen, lil possum, you're in the woods not chipotle."

"Alright, I'll do beans."

I put a can of beans and a can of corn over the fire for us. I took a swig of a stool softener. I extended the bottle to him, but he wasn't up for it.

"I have been in a deep state of contemplation. I am going to begin writing soon. I understand things now that I didn't before."

"Did you read all those books?"

"Just finished yesterday."

"Do you have magic eyes now?"

"Maybe I am not sure. Do you have magic eyes? How would you know?"

The can of beans were done. I handed them over to him. Then grabbed my corn. I only had one spoon. So I let him use it. I just dumped the corn into my mouth.

"You aren't going to come back are you?"

"No. I am not."

"I can't say I blame you. Can you at least just keep your phone on? Or agree just to call me once a week? We can make Sunday phone calls our thing."

I didn't say anything. I had learned so much, but I still had no idea how to be there for people. I just ate my corn. At some point I just said, "I have to think about it.". That was the truth. I had to think about it. The only structure I had had to my days was Kaitlyn. I had no idea how to introduce something else into my mental space. Someone else for that matter.

"I have been working on a song."

"Yah? Can I hear it?"

"Really?"

"Yah! I haven't heard a song in…..Lil Possum, how long have I been in the woods?"

"Just about a three years."

"Huh. That long."

The only thing that was heard between us was the owl. The sun had just slipped away and night was upon us. He ran over to his car and grabbed his guitar. He came back with it and a half-drunk bottle of Jack Daniels.

"It's from the last party I went to. We might as well.", he handed me the bottle. I threw the lid into the fire and took a swig. Handed it over to him and he took one too. His grimmace amused me. When did my baby become a man? He positioned the guitar and tuned two of the strings.

"This is a song I wrote for Yaya. It's different than writing, I guess, it's more following an emotion. You write to replicate scenarios that evoke certain things, I am trying to make a sound of the certain thing. I guess. I would concentrate on her and follow the feeling. I haven't come up with lyrics so I am just going to play."

He began playing. It was mainly plucking in D Major. The sound was melancholic and refined. As I listened and stared at the fire, memories of my Yaya giving my baby a blessing in Greek. Again when he was a toddler. Continuously throughout the years until she died.

I listened to the song and felt my grandmother's presence. Along the trail. By the water. In the grass. By the trees. When holding an acorn. She was right here with me in this moment and because she was in this moment—I found her presence in all of my memories.

When the song ended we both yawned at the same time.

Ah! I've got it. Being compelled to act is a result of external obligation. A compulsion is to act as a result of internal obligation.

I took out some paper and began to write lyrics. Not very thoughtout. Very spontaneous. Once I was done I handed them over to him. His eyes began to water.

"This is perfect, dad. Thank you."

"Things will be different, I promise. The song is amazing. Yaya would be very proud."

He nodded his head and put his guitar back in the case. He took a swig from the whiskey bottle. Then I did. We went back and forth until there was nothing left.

"What's the most fascinating thing you learned from all those books?"

I thought the most fascinating thing I had learned was learned from a woman. Not a book.

"The nervous system of Octupie are so advanced that some scientist have reason to believe that their pain has characteristics of suffering to it. While other species may experience pain more like a survival response, an octopus could be despairing over that pain. Some make the argument that this enough to believe that they are conscious beings. Other scientists suggest that the nervous system of Octupie lack the necessary components to even experience pain at all. That we should be okay with experimenting on them because they wouldn't feel anything."

"What do you think?"

"I don't know. I have never been an octopus."

We stared at the fire. Until it started to get late. We agreed to sleep in the tent together. I had not shared my tent with anyone before. Except for his mother many years ago. We are laying shoulder to shoulder.

"Dad.", he whispered.

"Do you ever get scared out here by yourself?"

"Fear isn't real."

"Right."

A few more seconds went by.

"Dad?"

"Yah."

"Why did you leave the first time? When you found out mom was pregnant with me?"

So he knew. Smart little bastard.

"I need to prove I was man enough."

"And now?"

"What about now?"

"Why did you leave this time?"

"I wanted to write the project that got me remembered."

A silence came over the tent. You could hear that owl that nobody ever saw. I wondered how far it was from here to Utah. I used to know, but now I don't remember.

Cobalt Silence

"This is the way,", said the elder to the younger, "it is the way now for it is what was. All must pass so that what may come will be received. Do not maintain the truth that is and was, then the great eagle will come and pluck the sight from your eyes.". This is the way. My face is the younger. My face is also the elder. My face is the women of my tribe. My face is the men. My face is the ancient soothsayers that have released themselves. They are not, so that we may. They are all of me. My face is all of them. My face looks to my palm and it is the palm of the elder. The mirror shows my face and the ears of my sister. My face is the elder. My face is my sister.

The elder continued to speak. My face was silent but was also the face that speaks. My face listens. My sister and my face sat while they stood. We sit and stand.

"Do not fill your heart with anger.", the elder continued. This elder was all of us. We are all of them. Their face is called Sheathed Saber. Sheathed Saber is a well-respected face in our community. They have sharpened their blade for a lifetime. My face has sharpened my blade for a lifetime. We become what we pay attention to. This is the way. They are famous for their diligence, resolve, and strength. My face is diligent. My face is resolute. My face is strong. We look to my sister. She is me and my face is her. Her face is called Narrow Path. My face is called Dented Shield. We are diligent. We are resolute. We are strong. We have much to learn.

"To fill your heart with anger, is to confuse the senses. To confuse the senses is to confuse the way. Do the mighty hounds of the leafless forest howl at a moonless sky?". My face could not answer the question, we had asked ourselves. For though my face was the elder, my face was also bound by the youth of my senses. Bound the way the staffs were bound in the hands of ancient warriors. Bound the way the leather wrapped around the sticks propping up our huts. It isn't until my witness has been consumed by the moon for the tenth time, that my face may actualize. When the moon would eat the sun, and life is painted with death. Every eighteen full faces of the moon. For the moon was pure death when it consumes the sun, but when the moon held the stars, it reflected sight through the darkness. It was only when death consumed life was it time for rebirth, but death alone illuminated danger and was wedded with silence. Nighttime became the ideal time to contemplate life, for life on the cusp of death is the truest form. We are always a heartbeat away from the silent symphony. This is the way.

The days of our birth are irrelevant to Pamarotu culture. Our witness is merely the returning of life from within to outside through pain. Pain requires a face to understand it. The same for pleasure. For all life from inside to outside, a debt must be paid to the sun. Pain and pleasure is the release of light. The sun returns to the earth from which all flowers must come. The sun is the great flame, the source of our face is flame, subtle like an amber, for this reason tears burn as they stream your cheek. The release of the source is always fluid. This is the way.

"Do we remain silent for we do not know the way or we wish to disrespect us? ", the way said through Sheathed Saber's face and voice. "To disrespect others is to disrespect oneself.". He borrows it from the moon and the sun, so that they may communicate their wisdom. Narrow path is confused. Her face has only seen five consumptions. This will be my face's tenth.

Every ten consumptions, through the tribe's reunion, the way abandons our faces and returns with the light of the sun. It is then we must see through our ears. Listen to our eyes. Smell through our lips. Taste through our nose. It is then the way reveals the new name for our face. We must touch within, by returning blood to the soil. We are meeting with Sheathed Sword so that the wisdom of the moon and the sun may prepare my face for what it must do. Narrow Path is here to bear witness, for one day she must do the same to her face, and she must understand that it is just a face. That she is not it. That she is nothing. That she is everything. That she is the death of my face. That she is also it's rebirth. This is the way.

"Well!?", Sheathed Saber's face containing the marks of many consumptions, wrinkled and scared, like the clay of our earth. These were symbols of wisdom for other faces to understand and respect, but some faces said Sheathed Saber contained too much of the way for one face. They scold us over the dangers of anger, and yet they wield the way with behavior like that of our stone smasher that wears the face of our creator. All the men who made us were the sky. All the women who gave birth to us were the earth. The soil and the trees that sprouted from her. The birds flew in his mind. The faces of our creation were seen as the voice of the sky and the earth until our tenth consumption. After the tenth they are us and we are them. They are already us but we become them after our tenth consumption. To allow us to become them, they must participate in the ritual, releasing us from their grasp so that we may rid ourselves of our past and our adolescence and become.

"Great elder, we can not know the way, we can only be the way. This face knows not the fate of great wolves in the leafless forest, for my witness has never been beyond our village. To speak when not knowing is to not know the way. Silent when ignorant is the way.".

The tips of Sheathed Saber's fingers touched their tired face. Their nipples looked down to the ground. The hairs on their neck looked up. They grabbed the great saber from the wall of their wicker hut. We sat about the fire. We stood about the fire. My face grabbed the blade. My face listened.

"Does your face see this?"

"My face only sees the way."

"Very good."

Their back was turned to us as the blade was held. Then, without warning, my witness sees a contraction of the muscles in their back. The movement was sharp, which means it was balanced. To be balanced is to act with courage and humility while containing the same face. My youth contained the silent serpent, all youth did. To be tempted and to be venomous is youth. This is our flame's spirit until the first commencement. Our next flame is revealed through our faces' new name. Revealed through the name and the interpretation of the elder's who have contained the moon and the sun for many consumptions. This is the way.

The blade came whistling in my direction. The muscles on their arm, despite being harnessed by the flame of a turtle, displayed the vitality of youth. My face does not contain the turtle. My face saw the blade through each individual drum of the heart. This is the way.

My chin to my knees as the blade passed overhead. The serpent strikes, bringing my heel inches from Sheathed Sword's face and with fingertips catching the blade before it lays waste to Narrow Path.

"Your training has come a long way."

"Every day is an opportunity to reveal the will of the tribe through my actions."

"This is the way."

"This is the way."

"This is the way."

"My bones tell me you are ready. My blood tells me the consumption will happen tomorrow."

My face's pride got in the way of my flame, "Has your blood ever been wrong? What of your bones?", as I returned to resting upon the soil. Their stare was sharper than the blade they had spent a lifetime sharpening. Before my face could sense anything, their movement was one with the wind, the palm of their foot struck the chest. The back crashed upon the wicker wall. My face could sense the light burning through the marks that were made.

"What is to doubt!?", roared the elder. In their fourth consumption, they contained the spirit of the lion. It was only then did he cease, and they became. For all know that Lion's travel in prides. This is the way.

"To doubt is to be an enemy of the way."

"Louder!"

"To doubt is to be an enemy of the way!", rising to my feet. Now their fist lay waste to my face. The light burned and immediately swelled as I covered the mark with my face's dirty palm.

"Do not step to me like you are a warrior! The way of the warrior ceased with the man who showed me the wisdom of the sky! Now louder!", they screamed and then suddenly made themself as small as their whisper, "What is to doubt?".

"TO DOUBT IS TO BE AN ENEMY OF THE WAY!"

"Are you an enemy of the way?"

"no..."

"What!?"

"NO!"

"Yet you doubt my face?! Does my face not contain the way!?"

"Of course, it contains the way."

"Ah, then you are an enemy of the way!"

"No, my face is mistaken. All faces are just mirrors of the way. Each mirror forged with time, forgive my witness, ancient soothsayer, my face is still forging."

My face looked towards Narrow Path. Her gaze was unwavering toward her toes. Violence and shouting makes her flame dwindle greatly. Experience tells my face it is true. The fear for her face was greater than my frustration and curiosity. The serpent of my flame began to swallow it's tail.

"On a white sandy beach, beyond the sea of love, is where the turtle came to me and removed this blade from it's shell. Then my face awoke from it's slumber and the blade remained in my bed, where the warmth of my flame used to lay her head. My flame dwindled and the darkness of desperation made me foolish. Mistakenly my face gave the blade to my sky, the Pamarotu's last great warrior. Do not dare speak the name of his face! He contained such great wisdom, my face thought it best, he have the blade. He would do what was right, is what my darkness told me using the voice of my flame. My face could not be more mistaken. The sharpness of the blade inspired a bloodlust through doubt. He doubted the way and lead some of the other men beyond the mountains, saying he had visions of a glimmering stone that would provide more than the way could. He was a great poet, and temptation is most dangerous to those with the insatiability of poetry. To seek more than the way is to already have less. They rode the ostriches beyond the mountainside. To leave our village is quite simple, but to return is impossible. The group of ostrich men left and never returned. The grinds from our coffee tell us they drank the blood of lizards out of thirst and became lizards under the moonlight. A punishment of their greed is to live the remainder of their days with the passion of man in the slow pace of the lizard. Does your face understand why it hears this legend?"

"Legends are to be experienced, understanding comes with time. This is the way."

The elder smiled. My face smiles. Narrow Path smiles. When the way smiles, the moon and the sun are in balance. As are the sky and the earth. The sea of love and the leafless forest.

"This blade," they said looking at it with great ambition, "was rediscovered while I was away grieving the loss of my warmth. Her flame was a canary and the bird visited me in a naked sunrise. The song released a great deal of light for my face knew it was hers. The song soothed my flame and restored its ability to guide. My witness followed it with obedience, absent any doubt, though my face did not know where it was going, it knew that it must trust the way beyond doubt. For to trust the way is to be the way. Eventually, beyond a path of lizards, at the top of a mountain was this blade driven into the ground. With great strength my face removed it and while holding it again, my face experienced the wisdom the dream turtle tried to bestow.", he swung it up directly. The light from the fire reflected off the obsidian. A blade as dark as midnight. As sharp as dawn. With a handle made of green ribbon like the shell of a great turtle. My snake told me to steal it. To swing at the warriors of my imagination. "Would you like to experience the wisdom the blade bestowed upon me?"

My face and Narrow Path nodded vigorously. "Of course, you'd like to experience, but does the way compel you to experience.". Sheathed Sword was providing us a moment for contemplation. My witness touched within. Felt the wind of my moon. The soil of my sun. My snake vomited it's tail and laid an egg.

"It is not our face's choice to experience or not experience. All we may do is receive. This is the way." [Artist note: Everytime I have encountered this line I cannot help but laugh. It's remarkable to me the ways I can be blatantly aware of the things I struggle with and still struggle to change.], spoke the voice of Narrow Path. We speak when she speaks. She listens when we listen. This is the way. Sheathed Sword looked at Narrow Path and allowed for the turtle to speak to her flame through the eyes. Hers was a silent doe.

"This sword's name is truth. A competent wielder of this blade can know great strength. This sword's name is honesty. To strike another with it is to know great humility. For all faces and all things are mirrors. To strike another is to strike oneself. This is the way."

"This is the way.", all voices became one voice.

"This is why we train. To wield but to never strike."

"Sheathed Sword?"

"Yes, Dented Shield."

"My sky tells me that this was not always the way. That there was a time, many faces ago, where our village was great. That we used our spears to slay the lizard people while on the backs of our ostriches. That the way was to strike those faces who had lost the way, and allowed doubt to traverse on to this side of the mountain."

"Your face speaks of truth. For all that is spoken, is the word of the way. Many faces ago, these palms that belonged to my face, my moon and my sun, my sky and my earth, knew the quench of blood."

"If all things that were must remain, and we do not strike down the enemies of our village, are we not in obedience with the way."

"Your face is wise beyond your consumption, but this is no longer the way."

"How can this be so?", spoke a silent voice from a distant corridor. Narrow Path's face was curious. My face is curious. Sheathed Sword is curious.

"To doubt me is to doubt the way."

"Sheathed Sword. Please."

Sheathed Sword's shoulders dropped. They contained the weight of every stone they had smashed.

"We fought with staffs then."

"What difference does it make if we fight with staffs or obsidian!?"

He sat. The night in his color expanded.

"For obsidian may be the truth and strength—honesty and humility—we know not it's source."

"The source of all things is the way."

"To doubt is to corrupt. Though the source of all things is the way, even doubt is the way unexpressed. One should step gently when the floor is known to crack."

"To step gently is to still risk walking."

Sheathed Saber burst out into laughter. Rolling back and slapping his face's knee.

"You are wise, Dented Shield, my face longs to see how you change."

And without answering any more questions the lesson was complete.

"Do not forget to tell your sky and your earth that you see them."

They proclaimed as we left their hut. Our sky was arriving at the same time we were. His face's hands were calliced and bloody from a long day of smashing stones.

"My sky if you know the ocean and the earth. The mountains and the leafless forest. Why do you pass your days smashing stones?", asked Narrow Path.

"It is true what you speak, young Narrow Path. My face has eyes that have seen the oceans, the great plains, the mountains, the leafless forest, and the place where the sun burns too greatly for the soil to drink in time. Where the moon brings in the tides before the soil may dry. And yet my choice is to smash stones."

"Yes. It is your choice, but why not choose something different."

"If it is not my face then it is another. My face has it's warmth in your earth. My face doesn't need more. This is the way."

"She has had enough lessons for the day, Righteous Fist, leave her be and get washed up. Supper is ready soon. Dented Shield, what says you of your coming consumption?", said my earth. Her face's name is Hushed Wave. Her face was a fitting representation of the earth for when I looked at her she was surely the singing birds, and the gentle breeze, and walking rain, and buzzing bees. We ate. The meal was when we'd know that the way was expressed the same. Different spoons, same flavors. It was in these brief moments where we allowed ourselves to come before the way. To embrace.

We slept. The reeds of grass sung in the wind. One could hear the silence of the bright darkness. A face was waking. A face was sleeping. A face would never wake again. Twas the night before my face's tenth consumption and my face saw visions in my sleep. Such violent and true visions that trying to recount them is dishonest. The one thing that was clear, my hand reached for the obsidian and my face heard one distinct question, "What color is invisible?". My face woke in a sweat.

"The Consumption will be at midday! The canary in the willow tree has spoken.", announced the face of Sheathed Saber to the many faces of the way. "It is Dented Shield's tenth consumption. We witness the death of our friend and watch the way give life to a new one.". The many faces of the way looked in my face's direction. My face nodded.

Righteous Fist placed his face's heavy paw on my face's shoulder. "Come with me my life.". My sky walked beyond the camp and my face followed, never looking away from the valley in his face's back. Such strength and he chose to smash stones. Some choies make themselves, whispered the way.

This is the power of warmth. The grass path went away from the mountains and toward the plains. My face could hear a running creek as the palms of my feet ceased upon the earth and felt the cool softness of the blue grass. We walked upon the grass for some time, until we began to climb, the stones were loose and one must use your face's hands. The creek that ran beside us was flowing away, we were heading up against the current. As our face's pressed forward the roar of water became immense. Growing in sound and anticipation. Finally we arrived at a small pond beyond the trees, it's source was a series of small waterfalls. Here the water was fresh, and the stones were sturdy. The color of their green reminds my face to consider how to step. This is the way.

Finally, my sky leaped on to a large stone with the agility of a face with still few consumptions. My face followed his lead, we sat and watched the falling water. Sitting there, our legs crossed, our flame became the water, both still and rushing and falling and crashing and still. A puma came leaping down from the trees. Their eyes were orange. My face began to unfold, ready to dart for the slippery stones, but before that my sky placed his hand on my thigh. The rest of his body had not moved. The puma showed him their teeth. It exhaled and it continued to walk by. It drank from the water that had become both of our flames. It turned and walked away. My sky said nothing and after some time he rose, walking back down the blue grass path.

As the path began to transition from blue to mud my sky followed the horizon elsewhere. We cut through trees and bushes until in the middle of pure distraction was an open field. We walked to the center and laid on our backs. The celeste dome of our being seemed so silent and so profound. Nothing more than what it was, but it was everything that it is. A vigilant hawk flew and began to circle, painting the sky with it's path. What color is invisible? The question of night visions plague my witness. My witness could see it's path painted along the celeste of our being, though it was not there. Only my face and my sky. The hawk was accompanied by the great eagle; they danced for some time. Do fish fly in the great ocean? Do birds swim in the great sky? The eagle dove beyond our vision and my sky flinched to pursue it, but my face rested my palm on his chest. His face looked at mine and smiled. "Do not fear what is to come. Your name may change, but your face will remain. Be one with the way and you will be great.". It was all that was said. The sun being approached by the moon, we understood that death was upon us. No time to lay in the pastures. Rising; this time he followed upon the forgotten path. My face now knew the way.

The village was outside, gathered in silent meditation, their faces pressed to the earth in the direction of the sun. The consumption was upon us. As my face passed them, they sprung to their feet and wiped the soil from their face. Then began to spit on their dirty palms. They rubbed it together and spat again. Then they dropped to their knees and showed their palms to life as it was consumed by death. The clear day was being consumed by the flames of death and nightfall. Our flames were dwindling. Sheathed Saber was there with a spear, their face painted in beautiful colors of mango and sea shells and sleepless nights and dormant days. Their strength was eclectic and mysterious. They were the way in it's purest. To his left was my earth. Narrow path was on her knees with muddy palms. She was still as she wept. "There is nothing to fear.", my face told her. My face told myself.

"OOOOooooo", Sheathed Saber began to sing from deep in their belly. The rest repeated. My face knew the power of the chant by being one of it's many voices, but now as my witness is upon death at the center of their semi-circle, my face became nothing but life. Deny my face this body, so powerful is the way, my flame bursts at the seems. It can barely be contained. My sky and earth look at Sheathed Saber with pity and they nodded with understanding. They stepped before me. My sky to the right of death. My earth to the left of life.

"OOOooWAYkeetocaminata!", bellowed Sheathed Saber, slamming his staff to the stone.

"OOOOOWAYKEETOCAMINATA!", the many of faces of the way echoed and filled me with strength. They slammed their fists to their chest then their thighs to the rhythm of Sheathed Saber's staff.

"dIEaNEW!"

"DIEANEW", the many faces of the way; a force as great as the wind.

"AWaaaay! aNEW!"

"AWAAAAY! ANEW!", the sound was as immovable as the mountains.

"CaminARR! NavigARR!"

"CAMINAAAR! NAVIGAARR!", they were a storm upon the great sea.

"Begin.", Sheathed Saber spoke as he gazed upon doom. The moon was moments from consuming the sun.

"Oooway!", then, "Heeeee!", with either a drum of the chest or a slap of the thighs between. My sky brought the blade to my face. He made a horizontal cut below my right eye. The rush of blood freed my face from the way and life. My earth took the blade and did the same below my left eye.

"LET THE DEATH OF THIS FACE BE AS GENTLE AS HIS REBIRTH!", screamed Sheathed Saber. My sky and my earth brought their lips to my wounds, they contained my blood in their mouths, they then dropped to their knees and spit it out. They mixed their hands in it, schmeared it to their faces. The moon completely consumed the sun. Even Sheathed Saber was upon their hands and knees showing the muddy palms to death. Facing it alone; this is when it began. With blood streaming my cheeks, the village went silent, all that could be heard was the distant singing of the reeds in the wind. It was a convulsion of ecstasy. My face was dead, but life had not returned. The flame that filled me needed to wrestle with the moon. It also needed to win.

In a complete surrender, my body stripped naked and began to howl, leaping and thrashing about. Fists laid waste to my own cheeks. Gripping and ripping locks of hair. Dropping to knees; claws peeled at chest. Life was there, just beneath the surface. As the light burst through from the right of the moon, the body panted and sweated, but did not cease to convulse. Leaping with all the force of the way. Scream. My face was returning. Scream! As life returned, my face tore it's throat to pieces. You may knock on my door, but you may never enter. Do you hear me?!

That's when the silence of life revealed it to my flame. Somewhere deep within, there was a snarling coyote. I collapsed to my knees. My flame suddenly was a forgotten candle in a distant cave. My earth draped my face with her cloak. The village rose to their feet. My sky gripped my hand and pulled my face in close. His eyes fought tears. His bloody mouth fought smiles. The village came and smeared the mud of their palms upon my chest. Narrow Path was crying as she did the same. My face pulled her in, "Hug me, my sister.", my face whispered in her ear. Her face wrapped her arms around my neck and held me tightly. In my face's exhaustion, a whisper more, "Tighter.". She squeezed tighter, the love from her flame was warm. Sheathed Saber commanded that my face stand.

"On his knees this face once belonged to Dented Shield, but as he rises to his feet this face is ever-new. We witness the death of a good man, so as to see the birth of the way in a better one. Rise! Tell us of your name!"

My face stood, upon legs that just sprung with life were now weak. The snarling coyote echoed somewhere within. "Tell us your name!", they proclaimed.

My face looked at my earth's kind eyes. My face looked upon my sky's proud smile. My face looked upon my sister's admiration. My face looked upon Sheathed Saber's contempt. My face felt the presence of those who had spread mud upon my chest. This was the way and though they had all gone through what my face had gone through, there was an assurance that this face contained wisdom that they didn't. "Cobalt Silence", rolled off my tongue.

It was as if my words made me the moon as it consumed the sun. My sky with one hand gripped his head and with the other reached to my earth. Her hands had begun to claw her cheeks as she collapsed, screaming in horror. Narrow Path became confused and ran into the arms of Sheathed Saber, who wore a heavy flame. The village walked backwards slowly; their attention tethered to my face. The wind that made the reeds sing became violent. Sheathed Saber released my sister from their grip and walked toward me slowly.

"Please! Not my child! Do not leave me! DO NOT LEAVE!", my earth screamed, clawing at her eyes. My name had caused madness in her. "Sheathed Saber, surely, he has made a mistake. He is too young.". Sheathed Saber placed his hand upon my sky's trap as to remind him that the way is beyond us all. "My earth! My earth! My earth! What is happening!? SKY!? Please!?", Narrow Path was running in place. Her tiny feet created a pitter patter that only added to the wind's violence.

"What is the spirit of your flame?", asked Sheathed Saber.

"The Snarling Coyote.", my face said it but there were no thoughts.

"NOOOOOO-a-a-a-AAAAAH!!", wailed my earth from the deepest recesses of her past. My sky quickly wrapped her in his strong arms. He then reached out for the other and shielded Narrow Path.

"You must annihilate your body or never come back. This is the way."

My face looked to my sky and my earth. "They are your mirrors now. Your face cannot look to them for guidance. This name that you contain is of a great warrior. You must leave and find your war before you bring it to our door."

"Where must my face go?"

"It must be at the mercy of your flame."

"If my flame commands that my face remain?"

"Then extinguish it."

"If it commands that my face walk?"

"Then move and do not stop."

"Weary Stallion!", shouted Sheathed Saber to the village medicine man, "bring me the obsidian blade and some molasses.". My earth contained herself and whispered something to Narrow Path. She looked to my sky, and he told her it was okay. She darted off in the direction of our hut. My sky kissed the forehead of my earth who was too weak to stand. He tore a garment from his pants and wrapped it around my face's forehead. Narrow Path returned with a satchel and a pair of moccasins. Righteous Fist tied a cloak about my shoulders. Narrow Path helped me put on our sky's old moccasins. He then placed the satchel upon my shoulder. Within it was a stone that one could hold in their fist. Some berries. A canteen with water. My earth's poetry, bound between leather cowhide. My sky's flute. Then Weary Stallion returned with the obsidian blade, he handed it to Sheathed Saber, then removed his straw hat from his head and placed it on mine. "Though the sun is life, too much of it will burn your skin. One face can only contain so much.". He then smeared the molasses above my wounds. Placing the rest of the cup in my satchel. It was then my face saw that there was my sky's tea kettle and my earth's tea pot, alongside a sack of herbs. Sheathed Saber was considering the obsidian they held within their hands. They swung it upward so the entire village may see the way the darkness cut and caught the light. They then sheathed it and tied it to my waist. They then kissed me on the mouth and said "Take the love of our village wherever you go and your blade will forever remain honest. You may go to the mountains, find the world of shining metals and greed, but then you may never return. Or you may see if you can cross the great desert, for beyond it is the leafless forest, and if you can survive it's mysteries you may find your way to the sea of love.".

My sky helped my earth to her feet, and they all gave me a hug. Things would be different now. My flame would not waver, but my face must learn to keep it warm from a distance. "The Snarling Coyote resides in the leafless forest. It will try to trick you. Listen to your flame.", my sky whispered in my ear. "Kill it. Be swift, it's life or yours.", whispered my earth. My face held Narrow Path one final time, "Don't go.", she said to me with tears streaming. "This is the way. If my face remains, then my face will surely die. This is my only chance at life. One day my face will remain with a new name and new stories. Be safe and be strong. Enjoy the good and the bad, it will all pass. This is the way.".

Without thinking, my face began to walk.

Twinkling sky, upon dying evening, life was absent—absent the sound of whole finches. Dust upon skin, left then right then within. Forgotten paths weren't meant for walkers intending on destinations, but there was no walker left to walk. Upon this path a choice was made, to the mountains and claim to fame or across the desert and into empty trees. Survival be thin like the smoke that hovers above flames, but if the choice be golden glimmer throughout golden hours within the choice was always illusion for the way is without doubt. Humility is the pride of the soul. Greed is the soul's price. A cobalt man in silent land headed toward the desert to discover what was right. Valleys of false god's were but the moon's distant sway. Canteens ran dry before there ran rain. The heat cracked the earth below the surface of one's face. If only there be words to eliminate the snarling coyote that contains no place. There is no such thing or deed or task or dash of grace, rather one's movement is the only way. Wicker hats and molasses cheeks, if not for there sweetness contained my face would loathe the smell of my body absent rain. The reeds of wind were in my past, but when the belly grumbled and the night placed blankets of invisible ice, my flame no longer flickered rather it blew out the songs of forgotten days. The seventh day of travel was the third of absent rain. The heat danced upon the horizon that no matter the movement remained ever distant. A great eagle swooped down before my dying dead body.

"Your conditions are weary and prospects are slim.", said the eagle to the dying man. With the strength that was left, we conjured a gaze that showed the eagle only knew the world from above.

"Don't you know that the way is false, and the only servitude you owe is servitude to him.", the eagle raised one of the claws, while balancing pointed a single talon. The belly rumbled to the rhythm of the horizon's quiver.

"Do you know the eagle's greatest strength is their sight? I can see your conditions for what they are and not what they ought to be. I must tell you, it is time you look within and wonder what exactly is the price for your life?".

There was a snarling coyote. The growl was as clear as the words that left the eagle's razor beak. "Eagles contain magic, the way all creatures do, to gain strength in the realm of their greatest virtue. I offer you a deal, I'll fly to the leafless forest from high up above, then beyond it to the white beach upon the sea of love. I'll scoop some of it's water into my beak and fly it into your mouth.", just as the deal was about to be sealed the eagle reached when saying, "I'll even give you the snarling coyote's whereabouts.". The fate of the journey had remained sealed, as far as the eagle knew my body was but a weary traveler desperate to make a deal, but he knew of the coyote the one that howls at the moon at night. The one that haunted hunger, the mountains, the desert, the fields. The one that in this body's dying moments, the distant sound was a reminder that destiny was real.

"No deal. No deal."

"Surely you will die out here unless you let me spit water inside. All I ask is that you let me look with your eyes. Your sight shall remain and look where you may, just know that if you accept the water then my flame shall remain hidden within your gaze. How else do you think I know about your past, without hearing you tell me; without having to ask?"

My sky gripped my body in the face of the puma; my body reached out in the pasture.

"No deal. No deal."

"You'll die!"

"One must be something to die, what is before you is nothing. Nobody. If this body ceases, then it has lived a life in which the destination of it's bones would remain a mystery. This is more than one can ask for. If death be the way then my face will know it's truth. This is the way."

The great eagle smiled, a sinister smile, one that hid joy that must remain unexpressed for to express it is to kill it. A smile that revealed to any spectator that it knew them well and that it would continue to know them. It raised it's wings as wide as it could, revealing smooth feathers beneath the spand. The feathers were a mosaic of different colors. Some feathers were shades of red and pink and orange and yellow and teal and magenta and burgundy and brown and black and white and all that fell in between.

"Pluck a feather and it will guide you on your journey.", before reaching there was noise. The snarling coyote was becoming increasingly present. "Which color is invisible?", the question was raised to the great eagle. The sinister smile grew but this time the wings flew to cover the eagle's beak. Not able to contain whatever was bursting at the brim, the bird bursted into the sky in a spiral of bliss.

Where the great eagle's claw had rested remained a single feather that was clear. Cobalt Silence picked up the glass feather and used it to bind the two ends of his cape. Though Cobalt Silence was just as dehydrated and tired as before, his interaction with the great eagle had returned warmth to his flame. His face had new vitality. The invisible feather, for some reason or another, his face understood that only him and the eagle could see it's outline.

Cobalt silence pushed forward. Each stride contained each previous one walked. The earth was now resisting the palms of his feet. The palms contained no fight and were pummeled by the weight of each stride. To journey with no destination can be a dangerous business. Yet Cobalt Silence had a goal. To find the snarling coyote that was a permanent resident of the leafless forest. To find him and kill him. This was to come for now he had to focus each stride on preceding the next while also fighting the heat. A blaring life shining down hard and bright. When cobalt silence mustered the strength to look ahead and see where his movement was guiding him he could see the waves of heat dancing upon the horizon.

Just when all was felt to be lost by Cobalt Silence he heard a running brook. Could it be real? Is his dying imagination playing tricks on his waking presence? Cobalt silence had been walking along the edge of a growing canyon for about twenty minutes when he finally found the source of the running water. Untying the straw hat placed upon his head it fell at the same time he did. Half of his torso was submerged in water. His dry lips swelled at the sensation of cool water. He chugged senselessly, not even considering whether the water was clean. It was cold enough and it's hydration was pristine. Nothing else mattered. After his belly was filled, he began to jump, sloshing around all the liquid in a celebration not allowing the flame to go out. Now he was dancing. Cobalt Silence was convinced that had he seen the creek two minutes later he wouldn't have made it.

"Follow the creek, through the canyon, and into the leafless forest. Be wary of serpents."

Cobalt Silence heard it in the voice of Righteous Fist but swore he had never heard his sky utter those words. The way works mysteriously and all he had was his intuition. So he filled up his canteen with water, took down a few more handfuls, and continued following the stream. A watchful eye near stones and plants where a serpent can hide.

Eventually he encountered not a serpent but a tortoise. It looked at Cobalt Silence. He remembered the legend of the blade he carried. He decided to sit with the creature. In silence the tortoise spoke of the history of the canyon. How this small creek was once a great river and each of the lines you see against the wall is where the river once ran. Before picking up the tortoise, Cobalt Silence asked the tortoise a question. Is the river the water or the basin?, he said. The tortoise smiled and reminded Cobalt Silence that he should be wary of snakes. All that was communicated between the tortoise and the man were through the eyes. This is the way.

The tortoise offered the man his shell in exchange for safe passage. There is a bend in the creek that is also the marker for the beginning of the leafless forest. Where clay transitions from it's red to a dead gray-green.

The tortoise spoke to the Cobalt's flame directly. About the way things were and weren't. What began with us and what ended with us. What we saw versus what we didn't see. And the boy now man listened with a patient ear for the tortoise was a terrific story teller but communicated slowly and softly. The tortoise was also very heavy and they were heading nowhere in no hurry. The boy informed the tortoise about his sky and his earth. About Narrow Path and Sheathed Saber. He excluded the tale of his name and new fate but the tortoise already knew. Though it hadn't been a significant amount of time, the man could not help but feel the distance between them. The tortoise listened to the stories and the distance offering earnest laughter and perspective. When they arrived at the bend the boy thought it was best to build a fire with twigs from the beginning of the forest. The tortoise thanked the boy for getting him there so safely and then retreated into the shell. The next thing the boy saw emerge from the shell was a black snake. The snake said take the shell and use it as a shield or a heavy fist. It would surely shatter, but it could deliver a necessary blow. The snake gave the man one final gift asking him to lean in. Cobalt Silence did and the snake bit his palm. The snake then told him to trust a snake to be a snake and a tortoise to be a tortoise. The snake slithered away into the impending darkness, while Cobalt Silence began to suck on the bite mark and spit out the venom.

That night, after removing the venom he smeared molasses and then bandaged his hand, immediately succeeded by collecting wood and building a warm fire. He had caught some mice and another snake. He squeezed the mice and beheaded the snake, cooking them on the same skewer. Cobalt read his mother's poetry. His favorite was the third, it was a poem about the moon and the stars. How they danced when the sun rose and remained still in the cold of night.

He ate the snake first and then the mice. The snake was tender like chicken and the mouse was gamey. This reminded him of the birds he used to eat. This made him think about the interaction with the eagle. He touched his glass feather and thought of his sky. Had the eagle tempted Righteous Fist in his youth? Maybe this was a path all must walk in the pursuit of greatness, which was merely the pursuit. To journey without destination, but he has a destination. To face the snarling coyote in the leafless forest. This was his fate but not his destination. A destination is a place of comfort where the mind may escape too. Fate was challenge's one faces on the route to themself.

That night he slung his hammock on two of the early trees. These trees could have belonged to the leafless forest or the canyon. They were stuck in between and Cobalt Silence thought it was his best bet. To be neither in just the canyon. Or just the forest. Rather to be partially in both while being in neither. This would keep him safe or he believed it would.

That night he had a dream. It was stranger than most and he blamed it on having eaten both predator and prey the night before. In the dream he had begun to pee at the foot of a dried basin. He peed so relentlessly that it began to burn. But despite his attempts to stop urinating he could not. It just continued to flow and flow endlessly. Eventually the tortoise turned snake appeared. It begged for forgiveness and safe passage. It was only then did pause to pee so that the snake could slither across the basin. When back on the other side he began to pee again. It was a gorge to a running river and the snake having crossed safely began to consume itself. Continually consuming it's tail until it could not further. It became a frozen circle that spectated the urine turning river.

Cobalt Silence rose with the sun. He packed his belongings from the fire and then sat in a smoldering contemplation. All dreams contain omens, he heard Sheathed Sabers voice. He removed the obsidian blade and it cut light. It's edge piercing the eye. Perhaps the omen will reveal it's truth with time. Perhaps. Time to move on. Destiny awaits. The snarling coyote must meet it's reflection.

He proceeded down the silent path. Each step was like a whisper as he made his way further and further. After spending the morning hiking inward, Cobalt Silence decided to pitch a tent. For he remembered his sky talking about the hunt, "in order to capture a predator you must become prey.". So, he pitched his tent between two trees. Built a fire at the mouth of the tent and sat. There he'd wait for three days and two nights. In a state that isn't quite sleeping, but similar to dreaming. In a state that wasn't quite waking, but similar to wandering. There he remained idling with a blade in his lap. Allowing the moments to come and go. This is the way.

In his waiting he had visions of Sheathed Saber, his sky, his earth, his sister, and all the tribe partners. He had visions of the turtle, the snake, his dream, the great eagle, and the puma. Most of all he had visions of the snarling coyote. He interacted with those visions with a distant admiration. For all enemies and friends are benchmarks. The greater the adversity the greater the individual. All enemies should be admired and overcome with grace. There was nothing personal in his duel with the coyote, it was simply the draw of fate.

But on the third night, fate had rung her bell. There was a tree that had collapsed down a drop off from the silent path. From the edge the coyote gently descended. Snarling ferociously. The mouth is foaming. Cobalt Silence lifts the blade and pushes it into the ground. He then twist and rests himself in a kneeling position.

"You have come to slay me? Many have tried."

"I am not only many. I am also just one."

"And what one might you be."

"My face is called Cobalt Silence."

"I was once called this name. Many lifetimes ago. I too slayed a coyote. I have slayed many since. You are me and I am you. And yet we are nothing."

"We are everything. Today your form must change. My blade will be swift."

"When my form changes as will yours. No combat shall be had. This vessel has served me well. Bring your blade down on the nape. Lay waste to my being, just know that when this body ceases so will your flame. The only way to protect it is to follow the silent path into The Valley of Fog. In silence being the protector of the mist. Until your vessel runs it's course."

"Tell me of the beast my face will annihilate. By dawn I will choose."

"You grant me one more sunrise. I will tell you any tale."

Cobalt silence, was no longer Dented Shield, and had no specific interests to deliver. Rather all he could do was recite his encounters. The Coyote listened while continuously snarling, faint enough where the man could hear it beyond the crackling of firewood. When he had recited all that had occurred. The coyote shined light on his adventures.

"The puma was sent by the way to tempt envy toward your father. By not acting upon it the way bestowed love. The eagle was the way tempting you with greed. Both times you resisted so you were bestowed generosity. Your generosity made you encounter the turtle, for your patience the turtle gifted you with zeal. But your zeal made you proud so the snake bit you to give you humility. Your humility has provided you with patience. Now with all that you are and aren't, how will you respond to the anger that lays before you?"

"The choice was never mine to make."

He rose. Raising the blade and walking with consideration made his route along the fire. As he came closer the snarling became louder and louder. He locked onto those red eyes. The morning was navy blue. The sun hadn't fully risen yet but it's rays had pierced the darkest hour. There was a bird in a distant tree singing in fourths. One a little closer singing in twos.

The coyote leaped. Cobalt put his forearm with the shell of the tortoise forward. The teeth dug deep into the shell and before it shattered Cobalt was able to pull the coyote to the left. He was grazed by a claw going down the inner thigh. The shell was destroyed and the coyote faced him again. Cobalt placed the blade in both hands and squared his stance. He began to breathe concentrating all his energy in the palms of his hand. He raised the blade and stepped lightly towards the coyote. The coyote got real low looking to make a jump for the throat. Cobalt stepped closer until finally they leap.

The birds flew into an open sky. The blade fell upon the nape with a whistle. Molasses was spread on the thigh. The head of the coyote was hollowed and worn by our champion who was now nameless. The straw hat was left covering the vacancy of the headless body. He threw the sword on his back and made his way down the silent path. To protect what remained of his flame in The Valley of fog.

It is my sincere hope that as you have read these stories you discovered something. Anything at all will bring me abundant joy.

Help someone in need when you can.
Thank you for reading.

ruben encontrado
7/25/2024

:)

Made in the USA
Columbia, SC
19 November 2024

46446935R10067